SF

P9-DME-516

Classics of Modern Science Fiction

UNEARTHLY NEIGHBORS

Volume 8

Books by Chad Oliver

NOVELS

Mists of Dawn (1952)
Shadows in the Sun (1954)
The Winds of Time (1957)
Unearthly Neighbors (1960; revised 1984)*
The Wolf Is My Brother (1967)
The Shores of Another Sea (1971)*
Giants in the Dust (1976)

STORIES

Another Kind (1955)
The Edge of Forever (1971)

NONFICTION

*The Discovery of Humanity: An Introduction to
Anthropology* (1981)

* Classics of Modern Science Fiction

Classics of Modern Science Fiction

UNEARTHLY NEIGHBORS

CHAD OLIVER

Volume 8

Introduction by George Zebrowski
Foreword by Isaac Asimov

Series Editor: George Zebrowski

Crown Publishers, Inc.
New York

Copyright © 1984, 1960 by Chad Oliver
Introduction copyright © 1984 by Crown Publishers, Inc.
Published by Crown Publishers, Inc., One Park Avenue, New York, New York 10016, and simultaneously in Canada by General Publishing Company Limited
Manufactured in the United States of America
Library of Congress Cataloging in Publication Data

Oliver, Chad, 1928–
  Unearthly neighbors.

  (Classics of modern science fiction; v. 8)
  I. Title. II. Series.
PS3565.L458U5   1984   813'.54   84-1875
ISBN 0-517-55294-9
First Crown Edition
10 9 8 7 6 5 4 3 2 1

To all of the fowl creatures at Turkey City, who were gracious enough to accept the Old Man as an equal, notably:

Leigh Kennedy
Lew Shiner
Bruce Sterling
Lisa Tuttle
Steve Utley
Howard Waldrop
and, of course, to one other:
Neal Barrett, Jr.

Retrieving the Lost

by Isaac Asimov

THE HISTORY OF contemporary science fiction begins with the spring of 1926, when the first magazine ever to be devoted entirely to science fiction made its appearance. For a quarter-century thereafter science fiction continued to appear in magazines—and only in magazines.

They were wonderful days for those of us who lived through them, but there was a flaw. Magazines are, by their very nature, ephemeral. They are in the newsstands a month or two and are gone. A very few readers may save their issues, but they are fragile and do not stand much handling.

Beginning in 1950, science fiction in book form began to make its appearance, and some of the books retrieved the magazine short stories and serials in the form of collections, anthologies, and novels. As time went on, however, it became clear that the vast majority of science-fiction books were in paperback form, and these, too, were ephemeral. Their stay on the newsstands is not entirely calendar-bound, and they can withstand a bit more handling than periodicals can—but paperbacks tend to be, like magazines, throwaway items.

That leaves the hardback book, which finds its way into public libraries as well as private homes, and which is durable. Even there, we have deficiencies. The relatively few science-fiction books which appear in hardback usually appear in small printings and few, if any, reprintings. Out-of-print is the usual fate, and often a not very long delayed one, at that.

Some science-fiction books have endured, remaining available in hard-cover form for years, even decades, and appearing in repeated paperback reincarnations. We all know which these are because, by enduring, they have come to be read by millions, including you and me.

It is, of course, easy to argue that the test of time and popularity has succeeded in separating the gold from the dross and that we have with us all the science-fiction books that have deserved to endure.

That, however, is too easy a dismissal. It is an interesting and convenient theory, but the world of human affairs is far too complex to fit into theories, especially convenient ones. It sometimes takes time to recognize quality, and the time required is sometimes longer than the visible existence of a particular book. That the quality of a book is not recognizable at once need not be a sign of deficiency, but rather a sign of subtlety. It is not being particularly paradoxical to point out that a book may be, in some cases, too good to be immediately popular. And then, thanks to the mechanics of literary ephemerality, realization of the fact may come too late.

Or must it?

Suppose there are dedicated and thoughtful writers and

scholars like George Zebrowski and Martin H. Greenberg, who have been reading science fiction intensively, and with educated taste, for decades. And suppose there is a publisher such as Crown Publishers, Inc., which is interested in providing a second chance for quality science fiction which was undervalued the first time round.

In that case we end up with Crown's *Classics of Modern Science Fiction* in which the lost is retrieved, the unjustly forgotten is remembered, and the undervalued is resurrected. And you are holding a sample in your hand.

Naturally, the revival of these classics will benefit the publisher, the editors, and the writers, but that is almost by the way. The real beneficiaries will be the readers, among whom the older are likely to taste again delicacies they had all but forgotten, while the younger will encounter delights of whose existence they were unaware.

Read—

And enjoy.

Introduction

by George Zebrowski

*U*NEARTHLY NEIGHBORS (1960) was Chad Oliver's fourth novel and his fifth book of fiction (counting 1955's distinguished short story collection, *Another Kind*). With it he closed a decade of impressive growth as a writer, by carrying forward his favorite theme of contact between intelligent species to a level of complexity and drama rarely seen in works of science fiction. "Chad Oliver continues to put his anthropology degree to good use," wrote Frederik Pohl. "Other science fiction writers have invented more 'alien' aliens than these for us to make contact with. Few, though, have been as able as Oliver to convince us that this is the way first contact is going to be." As humankind reaches out across the light years to confront another humanity, we see how both forms of intelligence are compelled to face their own inner natures before they can even begin to understand each other. Being alien, in Oliver's sensitive analysis, is not just a matter of physiological differences, but also a dimension of culture and history overlaid on the biology.

Sirius Nine is a vividly imagined world; its alternate humanity is satisfyingly complex and deeply felt. The anthropological puzzle presented by the planet's humanoid civilization is fascinatingly detailed, as are the lives of the investigators from our own future Earth. It's a wise novel, probing our deepest feelings as it strives to answer the question: what is a human being? In seeking the answer, Oliver's story faces us squarely with one of the central points of all literature—that mostly we do not know what we are under the overlay of civilization. There is nothing naively escapist about Oliver's fiction. I have never read a work by him that failed to provoke my feelings and jolt my thinking.

But even though he is not a writer of simple-minded adventure science fiction, Oliver's work is adventurous and exciting, even suspenseful and harrowing; no seeker of tense, absorbing narrative will be disappointed. His portraits of our culture-bound humanity at odds with itself gain intensity when alternate humanities (alien species) come on the scene. Oliver has no illusions about the worst in us even as he presents what could be better. His all-too-human protagonists always have to overcome their own inner failings as well as external problems. Oliver knows that we have not yet replaced given nature with a wholly successful creation of our own; in fact we may fail at this project of remaking ourselves and our environments and die off in civilization's wastes and warrings.

An outdoorsman and lover of nature, Oliver is also a romantic poet singing the subtleties of ecological-cultural adaptations. In this aspect his work has been compared to that of Clifford D. Simak. But as an anthropologist, Oliver shows

us man as a being who is trying to transcend the natural system in which he evolved. Can this creature continue to
adapt to its own changes or is it a hopeless exile incapable of
either accepting itself for what it is or changing itself into
something better?

Humankind, for Oliver, is an open problem of vast proportions, an unfinished project run by an intermittently en-
lightened artisan, humanity itself. Either we will learn
enough to help ourselves mature as a culture (we do this
better individually at this point) or we will remain on a kind
of historical treadmill (if we don't destroy ourselves). Combine this critical approach with an anthropologist's varied
insights and a writer's careful attention to his own individual experience and you have an author who stands directly
in the best tradition of a searching, probing science fiction—one in which, in the words of Anthony Boucher, "the
science is as accurately absorbing as the fiction is richly
human." This is the kind of writing that deserves the science fiction term, because it delivers on its full, genuine
meaning. Readers who discovered Oliver through his other
novel in this series, *The Shores of Another Sea,* have another excellent work awaiting them.

Unearthly Neighbors was first published as a paperback
original in 1960. The distinguished-looking Ballantine edition was well received, even though H. W. Hall's *Science
Fiction Book Review Index* lists only four notices (by P. S.
Miller, Leslie Flood, S. E. Cotts, and Frederik Pohl). It was
not a great year for science fiction publishing. *Unearthly
Neighbors* did not receive a British edition, and there was

only one translation. For this new edition, the author has made substantial revisions in the early chapters and various corrections throughout the text, thus making it the definitive edition of his novel; and this is the book's first hardcover appearance anywhere.

Classics of Modern Science Fiction

UNEARTHLY NEIGHBORS

Volume 8

Before the End

HIGH ABOVE THE tossing trees that were the roof of the world, the fierce white sun burned in a wind-swept sky.

Alone in the cool, mottled shade of the forest floor, the naked man sat with his back resting against his tree and listening to the sigh of the woods around him. He was an old man now, old with the weight of too many years, and his thoughts were troubled.

He lifted his long right arm and held it before him. There was strength in Volmay yet; the muscles in his arm were firm and supple. He could still climb high if he chose, still dive for the strong branches far below, still feel the intoxicating rush of the air in his face. . . .

He let the arm drop.

It was not only Volmay's body that was old; the body mattered little. No, it was Volmay's *thoughts* that worried him. There was a bitter irony about it, really. A man worked and studied all his life so that one day he would be at peace

1

with himself, all duties done, all questions answered, all dreams explained. And then. . . .

He shook his head.

It was true that he was alone, but all of the People were much alone. It was true that his children were gone, but they were good children and he could see them if he wished. It was true that his mate no longer called out to him when the blood pulsed with the fevers of the spring, but that was as it should be. It was true that he had only a few years of life remaining to him, but life no longer seemed as precious to Volmay as it had in the lost, sunlit years.

He looked up at a fugitive patch of blue sky that showed through the red leaves of the trees. He had walked life's long pathway as it was meant to be walked, and he knew what there was to know. He had not been surprised—except once—and he had not been afraid.

And yet, strangely, he was not content.

Perhaps, he thought, it was only the weight of the years that whispered to him; it was said that the old ones had one eye in the Dream. Or perhaps it had been that one surprise, that one glimpse of the thing that glinted silver in the sky. . . .

But there was *something* within him that was unsatisfied and unfulfilled. He felt that his life had somehow tricked him, cheated him. There was something within him that was like an ache in his heart.

How could that be?

Volmay closed his dark eyes, seeking the dream-state. The dream wisdom would come, of course, and that was good. But he already knew what he would dream; he was not a child. . . .

Volmay stirred restlessly.

The great white sun drifted down the arc of afternoon. The wind died away and the trees grew still.

The naked man dreamed.

And—perhaps—he waited.

$$\boxed{1}$$

FREE WILL?" MONTE STEWART chuckled and tugged at his untidy beard. "What the devil do you mean by that?"

The student who had imprudently expressed a desire to major in anthropology had a tough time in choking off his flood of impassioned rhetoric, but he managed it. "Free will?" he echoed. He waved his hand aimlessly. "Well—uh—like, you know."

"Yes, I know," Monte Stewart leaned back precariously in his ancient swivel chair and stabbed a finger at the eager young man. "But do *you* know?"

The student, whose name was Holloway, was obviously unaccustomed to having his glib generalities questioned. He fumbled around for a moment and then essayed a reply. "I mean that the—um—bottom line is that we have the ability to choose, to shape our own Destiny." (Holloway was the type that always capitalized words like *Fate* and *Destiny* and *Purpose*.)

Monte Stewart snorted. He picked up a dry human

4

skull from his desk and flapped the spring-articulated mandible up and down. "Words, my friend, just words." He cocked a moderately bushy eyebrow. "I will pass over a cheap shot at the derivation of the name *Holloway*. What type blood do you have, Mr. Holloway?"

"Blood, sir? Why—type O, I think."

"Let's be positive, Holloway." Monte Stewart was enjoying himself. "When did you make the choice? Prior to your conception or later?"

Holloway looked shocked. "I didn't mean——"

"I see that your hair is brown. Did you dye it or merely select the proper genotype?"

"That's not fair, Dr. Stewart. I didn't mean——"

"What didn't you mean?"

"I didn't mean free will is *everything*, not in biology. I meant free will in the choices we make in everyday life. Like, you know . . ."

Monte Stewart sighed and made a mental note to have Holloway do some nosing around in the history of sociobiology. He fished out a pipe from a cluttered desk drawer and clamped it between his teeth. One of his most cherished illusions was that students should learn how to think; Holloway might as well start now. "I notice, Holloway, that you are wearing a shirt emblazoned with an admirable slogan, slacks neatly trimmed off below the knees, and fashionably scruffy shoes. Why didn't you put on a G-string and moccasins this morning?"

"You just don't——"

"Your presence in my class indicates that you are technically a student at the University of Colorado. If you had been born an Australian aborigine, you would instead be learning the mysteries of the *churinga.* Isn't that so?"

"Maybe. I've heard about the revitalization movement in Australia. But just the same . . ."

"Ah, you have been paying some attention. We'll score that one a draw. Have you had supper yet, Holloway?"

"No, sir."

"Do you think that you are likely to choose fermented mare's milk mixed with blood for your evening meal?"

"I guess not. But I could, couldn't I?"

"Where would you get it this side of the Kazaks? Look, have you ever considered the idea that a belief in free will is a primary prop of the culture you happened to grow up in? Has it ever occurred to you that if the concept were not present in your culture you wouldn't believe in it—and that your present acceptance of it is *not* a matter of free choice on your part? Have you ever toyed with the notion that *any* choice you may make is inevitably the product of the brain you inherited and what has happened to that brain during the time you have been living in a culture you did not create?"

Holloway blinked.

Monte Stewart stood up. He was not a tall man, but he was tough and wiry. Holloway got up too. "Mr. Holloway, do you realize that even the spacing between us now is culturally determined—that if we were participants in a different cultural system we would be standing either closer together or farther apart? Come back and see me again next week and we'll talk some more. You might also reflect on the point that the timing of appointments is another cultural variable."

Holloway backed toward the door. "Thank you, sir."

"You're entirely welcome."

When the door closed behind Holloway, Monte grinned. Even with his rather formidable beard, the grin was oddly boyish. He had been having a good time. Of course, any moderately sophisticated bonehead could have given him an argument on the old free will problem, but Holloway still had some distance to cover in that regard. Nevertheless, the young man had possibilities. He just needed to unplug the computer now and then, stop coasting, and start thinking. Monte had seen it happen before—that startling transition from befuddled undergraduate to dogmatically certain graduate and, sometimes, on to the searching questions that were the beginnings of wisdom.

Monte enjoyed his teaching and got a kick out of his reputation as an old-fashioned fearsome ogre. Sometimes, he knew, he overplayed the role. He hoped that he had not been too forbidding with Holloway.

He moved over to the console, intending to punch up some data on the conversion factor in potassium argon dating for his class tomorrow. His short black hair was trimly cut, complementing the slight shagginess of his jutting spade beard. His clear gray eyes were bright and alert, and although he looked his age—which was a year shy of forty—he conveyed the impression that it was a pretty good age to be.

"Monte," he said aloud, "you're a damn fool."

He didn't need the data. Louise knew all there was to know about potassium argon dating; he could get it from her. Besides, his stomach was telling him that it was time to go home.

He locked his smoke-hazed office and rode the tube to the roof of the Anthropology Building. (It was not one of the larger buildings on the campus, having been built in the compact style that had come into favor early in the twenty-first century, but the status of anthropology had improved sufficiently so that it was no longer possible to dump the department into an improvised shack.) The cool Colorado air was bracing and he felt fine as he climbed into his copter and took off.

He did not know, of course, that Holloway would never be his student.

He did not even know much about tough choices—yet.

He lazed along in the traffic of the middle layer, enjoying the glint of snow on the mountains and the clean golden light of the westering sun. It had been a pleasant day, considering that it was a Wednesday.

He eased the copter down toward his rock-and-log home in the foothills of the mountains. He was surprised to see an unfamiliar copter parked on the roof right next to his garage. He landed, climbed out, and took a good look at it. The copter was a powerful machine. It had a discreet blue-and-white U.N. logo on its nose and official tags.

Monte did not exactly feel a chill of apprehension. However, like the man in the tall building who glanced up and saw King Kong peering in through his office window, he felt something more than mild curiosity.

The top door of his home opened before him, and Monte Stewart ran down the stairs to see what was going on.

The man was seated in Monte's favorite chair in the living room, enjoying what appeared to be a Scotch and soda. Both of these choices, in Monte's view, indicated a man of intelligence. He stood up when Monte entered the room, and Monte recognized him at once. He had never actually met the man, but his craggy face and silver-gray hair were immediately familiar to any tri-di watcher. Besides, Monte had seen him at close range several times when they were both involved with the NASA project.

"You're Mark Heidelman," he said, extending his hand. "This is an unexpected pleasure. I'm Monte Stewart. Was there some communication I didn't get?"

Mark Heidelman shook hands with a solid I-really-mean-it grip. "The pleasure is mine, Dr. Stewart. I always intended to introduce myself on that NASA business—you did one hell of a job. But I have to plead political sensitivities and all that. Sorry." He took a deep breath. "No, there was no contact with you. I just sort of barged in. It's rather shoddy procedure for a diplomat, but I *have* cleared things with your dean—crusty old bird, he is—and I've met with President Kovar of your distinguished university. She was quite complimentary about you, by the way."

"Ummm," Monte said. He hardly knew Kovar. "I take it then that this is an official visit?"

"It is, Dr. Stewart. Very hush-hush but very official. We don't want to start tongues wagging and this concerns your wife as well as yourself. Have I intrigued you?"

"You might put it that way." Monte waved him back to his chair and pulled up another one. "What's going on?"

"We're going to try to put you on a very sticky spot, Dr. Stewart."

Monte reached for his pipe, filled it, and puffed on it until it lit. Where the devil was Louise? He knew, naturally, that Mark Heidelman was the confidential troubleshooter for the secretary-general of the United Nations, which meant that he was a very big wheel indeed. The U.N. had gone through its ups and downs since the long-ago days of the near-legendary Dag Hammarskjöld, but now with its overt and covert operations it was as much an integral part of life as spaceships and taxes. The obvious question filled the room. What did the U.N. want with Monte Stewart?

"Please call me Monte. I take it that you need an anthropologist."

Heidelman smiled. "We need you, if that's what you mean. And we need Louise."

The servomec wheeled itself in, carrying a tray with two fresh glasses of Scotch and soda. It wasn't much of a robot—just a wheeled cart with assorted detachable appendages—but Monte and Louise had not had it long, and they were inordinately proud of it.

Monte took his drink, raised it toward Heidelman, and proceeded to indulge in one of the great benefits of civilization. "Now then, Mark. What's this all about?"

Heidelman shook his head. "Your wife told me that you hated to discuss anything before supper, and I'm taking her at her word. Anyhow, she was good enough to invite me to share a steak with the two of you, and she's doing the cooking herself. I'd hate to get booted out before I could do justice to the meal."

Monte chuckled, understanding more clearly why Heidelman was one of the world's most successful diplomats. The man radiated charm, and there was nothing at all unctuous or phony about it.

"Give me a hint, can't you? Mysteries make me nervous."

"You may develop some dandy ulcers before this one is

over with. Monte, one of our ships has finally hit the jack-pot."

Monte felt a cold thrill of excitement. He raised his bushy eyebrows. "My God, do you mean——"

With exquisite timing, Louise Stewart picked that moment to enter the room. Monte noted that she had activated her I'm-still-female-when-I-want-to-be role, which was a sure sign that she approved of Mark Heidelman. She had put on one of her discreetly sexy dresses, her dark hair was coiled in the latest fashion, and her brown eyes sparkled. She looked devastating.

"Steaks are on," Louise said. "I didn't cook them with radiocarbon, either. Let's eat." She gave Monte a light kiss on the forehead. "Monte, I'm about to pass out with curiosity."

"How do you think I feel? Let's get this show on the road."

They escorted Heidelman into the dining room, which was in a separate wing of the house. It was too cold for the roof to be rolled back, but the stars were clearly visible through the ceiling panels.

The stars. It had to be the stars.

Stuck with their own conventions, they managed to give respectful attention to one of life's most underrated pleasures: genuine sirloin steak, cooked to perfection. Heidelman did not insult the meal by talking shop. He waited until they were back in the living room and the servomec had done its thing by supplying them all with coffee.

"Okay," Monte said. "We've got a quorum and wonderfully stuffed bellies. No more messing around, Mark. About this jackpot you mentioned . . ."

Heidelman nodded. "I hope this doesn't sound unduly

melodramatic, but I have to say that what I am going to tell you is absolutely confidential. No matter what your decision, I know that I can rely on your complete discretion."

"Give it to us, man," Monte said. "Let's just pretend that we've run through all the preliminaries. What exactly have you got?"

Heidelman could not resist a pause for effect, but he kept it short. "One of our survey ships has found a planet with human beings on it," he said.

Monte tugged at his beard. "Human beings? What kind of human beings? Where?"

"Give me a chance, Monte. I'll spill it as fast as I can."

"Fine, fine. But don't skip the details."

Heidelman smiled. "We don't *have* many details. As you know, the development of the interstellar drive has made it possible for us——"

Monte got to his feet impatiently. "Not *those* details, dammit. We know about the stardrive. We know about the Centaurus and Procyon expeditions. What about these human beings? Where are they, and what are they like?"

Heidelman drained his coffee. "They were discovered on the ninth planet of the Sirius system—that's about eight-and-a-half light-years away, as I understand it. Maybe I was a little premature in calling them human beings—that's your department—but they look pretty damned close."

"Did you make contact with them?" Louise asked.

"No. We didn't expect to find any people out there, of course, but all the survey ships carry strict orders to keep their distance in a situation like this. We did get some pictures, and sensors were planted to pick up recordings of one of their languages——"

Monte pounced on the word like a cat going after a sparrow. "Language, you say? Careful, now. Remember that chimpanzees are very close to us biologically and they make a lot of vocal racket, but they don't have a true language. Even after a century of teaching them manual signs, there's a line they can't seem to cross. Language? How are you using the term?"

"Well, they seem to talk in about the same circumstances we do. And they are definitely not limited to a few set calls or cries—they yak in a very human manner. We have some films synchronized with the sounds, and several of them show what appear to be parents telling things to their children, for instance. How's that?"

Monte dropped back into his chair and pulled out his pipe. "I'll have to study the tapes. But if they *do* have a language, what about the rest of their culture? Things you could see from a remote position, I mean?"

Heidelman frowned. "That's the odd thing about it, Monte. The survey team was careful, but they were good observers. They couldn't see any of the things I would have expected. No cities or anything of that sort. Not even any houses, unless you call a hollow tree a house. No visible farming or industry. The people don't wear clothing. In fact—unless the survey was cockeyed—they don't appear to have any artifacts at all."

"No tools? No weapons? Not even stone axes or wooden clubs?"

"Nothing. They go naked and they don't carry anything with them. When they swing through the trees——"

Monte almost dropped his pipe. "You're kidding. Are you trying to tell me that these people brachiate—swing hand over hand through the trees?"

"That's what they do. They walk on the ground too— they're fully erect in their posture and all that. But with those immensely long arms of theirs . . ."

Louise laughed with delight. "This is too much! Show us the pictures, Mark. We can't take much more of this."

"Maybe that would be best." Heidelman grinned, knowing that he had his victims thoroughly hooked. He stood up. "I have some photographs right here in my briefcase."

Monte Stewart stared at the brown briefcase on his living room table with an excitement he had never known before. He felt like Darwin must have felt when he first stepped ashore on that most important of all islands. . . .

"For God's sake," he said, "let's see those pictures!"

2

THERE WERE FIVE photographs in full color. Heidelman handed them over without comment. Monte shuffled through them rapidly, his quick gray eyes searching for general impressions, and then studied them one by one.

"Yes and no," he muttered to himself.

The pictures—which were obviously stills blown up from several film sequences—were not of stupendous quality. They were a bit fuzzy and the subject matter was irritatingly noncommittal. The pictures looked like what they were: random shots of whatever had wandered into range.

Still, they were the most fascinating photographs that Monte had ever seen.

"Look at those arms," Louise breathed.

Monte nodded, trying to get his thoughts in some kind of order. Only five pictures, but there was so much to see. So much that was new and strange—and hauntingly familiar.

The landscape was disturbing, which made it difficult to get the manlike figures into perspective. There was nothing about it that was downright grotesque, but the *shapes* of the trees and plants were subtly wrong. The colors, too, were unexpected. The trees had a blue cast to their bark, and their leaves were as much red as green. (Autumn on Sirius Nine?) There were too many bright browns and blues, as though a painter's brush had unaccountably slipped on a nightmare canvas.

The Sun, which was visible in two of the pictures, was a brilliant white that filled too much of the sky.

The whole effect, Monte thought, was curiously similar to the painted forests one sometimes saw in old books for children. The trees were not quite the trees you knew, and the pastel flowers grew only in dreams. . . .

Of course, after the bleakness of the solar system, *any* trees and flowers provided a certain welcome reassurance.

"They are people," Louise said. "They *are*, Monte."

Yes, yes, he thought. *They are people. How easy it is to say! Only—what is a man? How will we know him when we meet him? How will we know her? Will we ever be sure?*

Superficially, yes—they were people. (And they were mammals too, unless females were radically different on Sirius Nine.) But Old Lady Neanderthal had also been part of the family, different only at the subspecies level. And even *Pithecanthropus erectus* belonged in the crowded genus *Homo*.

What is a man?

Monte's hands itched; he wished fervently that he had some solid bones to look at instead of these blurry pictures. For instance, how did you go about estimating the cranial capacity from a poor photograph? The skulls might be almost completely bone for all he knew; the gorilla has a massive head, but its brain is nearly a thousand cubic centimeters smaller than a man's.

Well, what did they *look* like?

The general impression, for what that was worth, was unmistakably hominid. The people—if that was indeed the word for them—were erect bipeds, and their basic bodily outlines were not dramatically different from earthly hominids—or at least hominoids. The legs, in fact, were very human, although the feet seemed to have a big toe sticking out at a right angle to the other toes. (Monte couldn't be sure of that, however. Unless the camera catches it just right, it's hard to see even on a chimpanzee.) The arms were something else again. They were extremely long, almost touching the ground when the people stood up straight. But the people were fully erect; there was nothing of the stooped posture of the ape about them. The bodies were hairless and rather slender, and the skin color was a pale copper.

Faces? Call them unusual, but within the human range. They were long and narrow, with relatively heavy jaws and deeply recessed eyes. Monte could not see the teeth, but it was clear that the canines, at any rate, did not protrude. The head hair was uniformly light in color and was very short—hardly more than a fuzz.

Heidelman's description had been accurate as far as it went. The people wore no clothing, but two of the men had vertical stripes painted on their bodies. The painting seemed to be confined to the chests and was quite simple—a streak of red and one of blue on each side of the chest.

None of the people carried any weapons.

Monte saw no tools of any sort and no houses. One of the men was standing in front of a large tree that appeared to have a hollow chamber in it, but it was difficult to tell.

There was a child in one of the pictures. He seemed to be five or six years old, if earthly analogies could be trusted, and he was hanging by one hand from a branch and grinning from ear to ear. A female was shaking her finger at him from the ground below, and the impression of mother and son was very strong—and remarkably human.

But then, of course, the mother-and-son relationship often seemed quite human, even in monkeys. . . .

Monte carefully put the photographs down on the table.

"Brother," he sighed. And then: "Brothers?"

Monte abandoned his pipe for a cigarette, which was a sure sign that he was worried. He began to pace the floor.

"I don't get it," he said. "You say that they do no farming, and yet they can't hunt because they have no weapons. So where the hell do they get their food?"

"Couldn't they live off wild fruits and roots and stuff like that?" Heidelman asked.

"It's possible, I suppose."

"Come on, Monte," Louise said. "Apes do it, don't they? And some of them hunt, too."

"Sure, but these people aren't apes—unless you want to call human beings modified apes, which *is* one way of looking at it."

"You're lecturing, Monte," Louise said.

"Sorry. But Mark says that they have languages, and that's a human characteristic no matter how you slice it. Forget about the ape hoots and whale whistles. If they have

languages, you'd expect them to have cultures too; cultures
and languages go together like Scotch and soda. I've never
heard of any group of human beings without any tools at all.
Even the simplest food-gathering peoples had digging sticks
and spears and baskets and things of that sort. Either these
people are the most primitive ever discovered, or else——"

Louise laughed fondly. "Monte! I never thought I'd
hear you say what you were about to say. After all your
caustic remarks about yarns involving primitive supermen . . ."

"The catch is," Monte said seriously, "that *primitive* is
a pretty slippery word. We think we know what it means on
Earth—it refers to a nonliterate culture without urban cen-
ters. The notion works fairly well here, but what can it possibly mean when it is applied to people on another planet?
We don't really know a damned thing about them or their
cultural histories, and fitting them into a ready-made cate-
gory derived from a total sample of one world may be a gross
mistake. As for supermen, I doubt whether the concept is a
valid one at all—are we superapes or are we something else
altogether? These people could be *different* without being
super, if you get what I mean."

Heidelman smiled a quiet, satisfied smile. "Of course,"
he said, "the only way to find out the truth is to go and see."

There were the words, the words that had to be spoken.
They were followed by a long silence.

Monte finally ground out his cigarette and lit another.
"Yes, yes. Is that what you want us to do—or am I supposed
to wait until I'm asked?"

"You *are* being asked. Do I have to wave flags and ring
bells? We want you to lead a scientific expedition to Sirius

Nine, and the sooner the better. We want you to start your planning *now*. We are determined to have a trained anthropologist make the first contact with these people—I'd like to think that we've made at least enough progress to avoid some of the more glaring errors of the past. How about it?"

"Just like that, huh?" Monte perched on the edge of a chair, feeling as though he had just been handed the gift of immortality. "Hell, of course I'll go. No need to waffle about it. But look, Mark, there are a couple of things we should get straight——"

Heidelman nodded. "I know what you're thinking, and you can relax. We know how important this is, and we're prepared to give you all the authority you need. You'll be pretty much your own boss. You'll be free to pursue any scientific work you want to undertake. All we ask is that you do your level best to establish a friendly contact with the people on Sirius Nine and make a full report to us when you get back. We'll expect you to make any recommendations you see fit, and you'll have a voice in seeing to it that they're carried out. You can select anybody you want to work with you. We'll supply a ship under Admiral York—he's a good man—and he'll get you there and be responsible for your safety. But in all relations with the natives you will be in charge. Your only superior will be the secretary-general. The U.N. will pay your salary and will arrange for you to take a leave from the university. Louise will also be on salary; we know that you'll need her to work out dating sequences. We can hash out the details later, but how does that sound?"

Monte was stunned. He had not, in fact, been thinking on such an exalted plane. He was close to being in shock, and his mind had seized on smaller questions: *Who will take over my classes? What about my graduate students? How about all the wretched committees, the curse of university life? Who will move into my house?*

He finally said: "Why me? I'm not the world's greatest anthropologist. There ain't no such animal anymore, not since the days of Boas and Kroeber. Shouldn't there be an election or something?"

Heidelman shook his head. "Impossible. I'll get to that, if it worries you. But I'll tell you flat out: this has not been a hasty decision. We want you because you're good and because you've got some sense. That's crucial. We know you and we know what you can do. That's crucial. As for who might be the world's greatest anthropologist—well, that's *not* crucial and we really don't give a damn. If you know such a mythological being, fine. Take him or her with you."

Monte tried to collect his flying thoughts. "It sounds too good to be true. There must be a catch in it somewhere."

"There is. You put your finger smack on it awhile back. We don't really know anything much about those people. It won't be an easy job, and it may very well be dangerous. I'm not going to try to minimize the danger. You'll be risking your life out there—and the life of Louise as well."

Monte shrugged. It wasn't that he did not have a high regard for his own skin, but staying at home now was completely unthinkable. He did not insult Louise by asking for her opinion; he knew his wife well enough so that words were superfluous.

"How long do we have?" Monte said.

"That's partly up to you. With the new stardrive propulsion, it will take the ship a little better than eleven

months to reach the Sirius system. If you spend a year on
Sirius Nine, that will put you back on Earth in about three
years if all goes well. We can stall things that long, I think.
We'll want to get going as soon as we can—I don't have to
tell you that if word of this leaks out there'll be the devil to
pay."

"Pardon our ignorance," Louise said, "but why?
What's the need for all the secrecy?"

Mark Heidelman smiled. He was in his element now.
"You are intelligent people, but you don't know one hell of
a lot about politics. This would be the news sensation of all
time. Once the people got wind of it, every government that
could throw a starship together would start a race for that
planet. Any chance of a genuine scientific expedition would
go out the window. Those people out there would be tried
and convicted a million times over by the media—either as
subhuman savages or as dangerous monsters. There's another possibility—they might be exploited as the saviors of
humanity, and half of the U.N. would insist that we genuflect out of respect for the Space Gods. There would be
power plays you wouldn't believe. There's a real chance for
a blowup here; you never know what's going to happen
when people get excited and start to calculate political ad-
vantage. We can't afford that. We've got to have accurate
information *before* this thing breaks."

Monte went back to his pipe. "What happens after you
get your accurate information, if you get it?"

"That depends on what you find out, doesn't it? After
all, those people may *be* dangerous. They could even be
gods, for all we know. We picked you for the job because we
think you're hard-headed enough to stick to the facts."

"It's a fantastic responsibility."

"Would you rather someone else had it? Who?"

Monte had no answer.

"I told you that you were headed for some ulcers. They go with the territory. This job isn't all cocktails and suave diplomacy, you know." Quite suddenly, Heidelman looked very tired.

Watching him, Monte had a flash of insight into the problems that faced the man. This Sirius thing, dramatic as it was, was only one of a vast series of interlocking and never-ending crises. It must have taken a mind-numbing pile of conferences before this job could even be offered to Monte. And at the same time there was the eternal task of keeping the U.N. afloat in a sea of distrust. There was the cute question of what to do about Brazil's insistence on testing atomic weapons. There was the border squabble in the Middle East. There were the renewed population explosions in China and India. . . .

"I think it's time for a nightcap," Louise said and called in the robot. With expert skill, she turned the conversation into quieter channels. Without ever actually saying so, she implied that the heavy discussions could wait until tomorrow. The world could survive that long.

Monte discovered that Mark shared his passion for trout fishing, and the two men got into an amiable argument concerning the relative merits of the Royal Wulff and the smaller match-the-hatch flies. They solemnly swore that they would try Beaver Creek together when Monte got back from Sirius Nine.

By the time Heidelman reluctantly went off to bed at two o'clock in the morning, they all had a slight buzz on and they were all good friends. That helps a lot in any enterprise.

While the robot clicked and wheedled around cleaning up the room, Monte began to prowl aimlessly, too keyed-up to sleep. Go fishing when he got back from Sirius Nine! It had been a crazy day. He felt like a stranger in his own living room. He looked at the familiar books and cassettes that lined the walls, frowned at the early-period Tom Lea painting that had always had a calming effect on him, tramped down the corners of the still-bright Navaho rugs scattered over the muted red tiles of the floor. This was his home. As an anthropologist, he was no stranger to departures. But only a few short hours ago his life had been comfortable, his future pleasant and moderately predictable. And now, with the suddenness that was one of life's most characteristic calling cards, it was all new and strange. . . .

Louise took his arm. "Let's go look at it," she said.

At first, he didn't understand her. Then he snapped his fingers.

Side by side, they walked over to the picture window and pulled back the drapes.

They looked out into a wintry blaze of stars beyond the black silhouettes of the Colorado mountains. Monte felt a brief shiver run through his wife's body.

"There it is," he said, pointing. "Funny, I even remember the name of the constellation: Canis Majoris."

"I wonder what constellation we're in," Louise said.

"I confess I never thought it would happen, really. After those completely alien things uncovered by the Centaurus and Procyon expeditions, the human critter seemed like a very unlikely accident. I was reading an article just the other day—remember, I told you about it—that estimated that there was less than one chance in a million for the independent evolution of manlike beings somewhere else. According to this joker's theory——"

"Theories! You know what you always say about theories."

"Yes. But it's a strange feeling just the same."

Strange, and more than strange. The light that took the picture I held in my hand a few hours ago won't reach the Earth for more than seven years. It is far, so far. . . .

He held Louise tightly in the circle of his arm. He was not afraid, but she seemed even more precious to him than before. She was all that was warm and thinking and alive in a universe vast and uncaring beyond belief.

"Well, old girl," he said quietly, "I'm glad you're going with me."

She gave him a playful kiss. "We're going together, dear. You don't think you were selected on your own merits, do you?"

They stood for a long time before the window that opened on the night, watching and wondering and trying to believe.

They could see Sirius plainly.

It was the most brilliant star in the sky.

3

H OW DO YOU go about setting up an expedition that is designed to make the first contact with an alien, extraterrestrial culture? Monte didn't know, for the excellent reason that it had never been done before.

Obviously, it was too big for the two of them. He couldn't just put on his boots and pith helmet and sally forth with notebook in hand. "Come, Louise. I will make penetrating observations and you calibrate the chemistry for the dating. Nothing to it."

Nevertheless, the other extreme was equally absurd: he couldn't take everybody who might have an interest in the problem. For one thing, that would have required a fleet of spaceships. (Lord, there would even have to be committees!) For another, unleashing a horde of investigators upon what seemed to be a relatively simple culture would have been a sure way of guaranteeing that no one would get any real work done.

Quite early, he decided on a minimal expedition. He would take the people he needed for the basic spadework and leave the more specialized problems for later. He told himself that he was motivated by practical considerations, which he was to some extent, but the fact was that Monte had a deep-seated suspicion of all massive and grandiose research schemes. Multiplying the number of brains working on a given job, he knew from long experience, was far from a surefire way of improving the quality of the final product.

Well, who did he need?

Monte himself was something of a maverick in modern anthropology. He was primarily a social anthropologist, and his major research had been involved with a search for regularities in the culture process. Characteristically, however, Monte hadn't stopped there. Impelled partly by a taste for the unconventional and partly by a conviction that biological and social anthropology belonged together, he had also made himself reasonably expert in the most technical field of physical anthropology, population genetics. (The thought of getting blood samples from the people on Sirius Nine made him as eager as any Transylvanian vampire would have been under the same circumstances.)

He needed a linguist. The whole shebang cried out for the best damned linguist available, and so Monte swallowed his personal feelings and chose Charlie Jenike. Charlie was a sour and faintly uncouth individual with a distinct resemblance to a dyspeptic penguin, and he had the quaint habit of wearing shirts for days on end until they virtually anesthetized unwary co-workers. Just the same, Charlie Jenike was a brilliant linguist. If anyone could crack one of the native languages in a hurry, Charlie could do it. Oddly enough, human animals being the strange creatures that they are, Charlie's wife, Helen, was a doll—tiny and dainty and singularly charming. She was also no mean linguist herself; the joke in the profession was that when Helen didn't work, Charlie didn't publish. Helen and Louise got on well together, which partially compensated for the sparks that flew when Monte and Charlie glared at one another over a supposedly friendly brew.

Harvard's Ralph Gottschalk was probably the best of the younger physical anthropologists, and he knew as much as any living person about the primates generally. In view of the rather gibbonoid appearance of the people on Sirius Nine, Ralph had to go along—and anyhow Monte liked to have him around for company. (Field rule number one: if possible, have somebody with you that you *like*. It helps when the going gets sticky, and it always *does* get sticky.) Ralph—a giant of a man with the build of a gorilla and the most gentle disposition Monte had ever encountered—was an unfathomable poker player and an eminently sane individual. Ralph was married to an enigmatic lady named Tina, and he invariably left Tina at home when he traveled. It was hard to say whether this was Ralph's idea or Tina's, but at any rate Ralph always seemed tickled to death to get away. In the field, Ralph tended to wear the secretive smile of a kid playing hooky from school.

If everything worked out according to plan—not that Monte thought for a moment that it would—a certain amount of psychological testing would seem to be imperative. Tom Stein's work in Micronesia had impressed Monte, and when he had met him for the first time at a meeting of the A.A.A. in San Francisco the impression had been strengthened. Tom was a tall, skinny guy, prematurely balding, with pale blue eyes that were almost hidden behind thick glasses. His shyness failed to conceal the fact that he had a razor-keen analytical mind; furthermore, although he was best known for his work in the culture and personality field, he had a genuine feel for social structure. He and his wife were inseparable. Janice Stein was a plain, rather dumpy woman with a radiantly pleasant attitude toward life. Many people underestimated her, but Monte was aware that she had designed some of Tom's most effective projective tests.

Finally, Monte picked Don King. It was a tough decision; Monte's first choice was Cal's Elizabeth Plascencia, but Louise insisted on Don King. She had worked with him before. Don was an archeologist, something of a lone-wolf in his ideas, and a decidedly sharp cookie. Monte didn't actually *like* Don—few people did—but the man was stimulating. He was a valuable irritant because he never accepted anybody's ideas at face value, and he loved an argument above all other things. Don, who was currently in his chronic state of moving from one sexual partner to another, was almost offensively handsome—a tall, well-built, sandy-haired man who habitually dressed as though he was about to pose for a fashion advertisement. Mark Heidelman had questioned the inclusion of Don, since the people of Sirius Nine did not appear to make tools, but Monte was certain that Don would pull his share of the load. A good reconnaissance ought to establish whether or not stone tools had been made in the past. In any event, the scanty pictures available were not a reliable guide, and if those people in fact lacked tools there was the key question of how they got by without them.

Eight anthropologists, then, to breach a world.

Presumptuous?

Sure—but (as Monte was fond of remarking) when there were no precedents you had to make up a few of your own.

The ship was a great metal fish of the deeps; it lived in space. Like the strange fish that live in the long silences and eternal shadows, the ship had never known the shallows that border the shores. It had been assembled in an orbit around the Earth, and its only home had been the vast seas of space and stars.

The exploration crew had been ferried up to the U.N. satellite and had boarded the ship there. The ship had flashed out past the Moon on conventional atomic thrusters and had then gone into the overdrive field that permitted it, in one sense, to exceed the speed of light.

By international agreement, all interstellar ships were named after human beings who had become symbols of peace. This one, officially, was the *Gandhi*. However, you just *can't* think of a tremendous sphere of hurtling metal as the *Gandhi*. Since it was the second ship to make the long run to the Sirius system, the crew, with the strained logic that sometimes filters up out of bull sessions, had promptly dubbed it the *Son of Sirius*. After some three months in space, the happy thought had occurred to one bright lady that Sirius was the Dog Star. From that point on, the evolutionary semantics were inevitable.

From Admiral York on down, everyone referred to the ship as the *S.O.B.*, although the polite fiction was maintained between officers and crew that the initials stood for "Sirius Or Bust."

Monte and Louise had found that packing for a trip to Sirius was annoyingly like packing for a trip anywhere. There were the same nagging problems about what to take and what to leave behind, the same soggy decisions about how to lease the house, the same frayed nerves and perpetual irritations. The force of habit was so strong that they even worked it out so that their departure took place between semesters.

When they finally got away, it was a relief; and the jump up to the U.N. satellite had been a wonder. The stars seemed so close that you could almost reach out and touch them, and the velvet abyss of space was a real and tangible thing. It was much the same feeling that a man had when he went to sea for the first time, and he stood on the deck with the wind in his face and looked out across the living green waves and the bowl of the sky and knew that the world was new and mysterious and anything could happen. . . .

Once they were inside the swollen metal bubble of the starship, however, it was all very different. It rapidly became evident that the voyage to Sirius was going to be something less than a volcano of excitement. Admiral York ran a tight ship, and he smothered the possibility of emergencies with a calm efficiency that took everything into account and corrected errors before they could happen. There was nothing to see and very little for a passenger to do.

When you got right down to it, Monte supposed, an interstellar spaceship was the least interesting way to travel that there was. He made the discovery that millions had made before him: that riding in a big jet, for instance, isn't half as much fun as flying in a small plane, and that for sheer joy no plane can compete with a horseback ride through beautiful country or a canoe trip down a clear stream leaping with rapids. The more exotic the mode of travel—spaceship, submarine, what-have-you—the more people had to carry their own specialized environment with them. Further, the more specialized the artificial environment, the less direct contact with the natural world outside.

The hyperspace field surrounding the starship might have been a mathematical marvel, but you couldn't see it, feel it, hear it, or touch it. Your world was *inside* the ship, and that was a rather barren world of gray metallic walls and fragile catwalks and cool, dead air that whispered and hissed through damp gleaming vents and endlessly circulated and recirculated in the vault that had become the universe.

Eleven months in a vault can be a long, long time.

Still, there was work to be done. . . .

Voices.

Monte leaned against the cold wall of the small boxlike chamber that Charlie Jenike had rigged up for his equipment and absently stroked his beard. He listened to the sounds that came out of the speakers and perversely tried to make some sense out of them.

It was impossible, of course. The voices sounded human enough; he could recognize what seemed to be words spoken by both men and women, together with utterances that sounded like the speech of children. But the sounds picked up by the hidden sensors of the first Sirius expedition conveyed no meaning to him at all. They were voices that spoke from across the immense gulf that separated one species from another, voices of people who were more remote from him than a Neanderthal from the last age of ice. . . .

"Doing any good, Charlie?"

Charlie Jenike twisted his aromatic form around on his stool and shrugged. Monte had the distinct feeling that he was about to spit on the floor, but he was spared that indelicacy.

"Good? I'll tell you something, Stewart. I'm right where I was a week ago, and that is precisely nowhere. Let me show you something."

"I'm all eyes. Or ears."

Jenike, moving with surprising grace and skill, set up a projector and fiddled with the computer that controlled the sounds from the speakers. "Got an action sequence here with a few sentences to go with it," he muttered. "Give you some idea what I'm up against."

A good clear picture formed in the air, sharp and three-dimensional. A male native of Sirius Nine dropped down out of the trees—there was a distinct thump when he landed—and walked up to another naked man who was standing in a clearing. The pickup was amazingly sensitive, and Monte could even hear the rapid breathing of the new arrival. The man who had descended from the trees said something to the other man. It was hard to catch exactly what he said, because the *sounds* of the language were utterly different from any language Monte knew. The man who had been there first hesitated a moment, then gave a peculiar whistle. The two men went off together and disappeared into the forest.

Jenike cut the equipment off. "Neat, huh? That's about the best we've got, too. I've worked out the phonemic system pretty well; I can repeat what that guy said without much trouble now. But what the hell does it mean?"

"What you need is a dictionary."

"Yeah. You get me one first thing, will you?"

Monte shifted his position carefully; the low artificial gravity field that Admiral York was so proud of was apt to send you smashing into a wall if you forgot what you were doing. He appreciated Charlie's problem. It would have been a tough nut to crack even if he had been working with a known culture.

Suppose, for example, that two Americans meet each other in a hallway. Imagine that for some reason they speak in a private language that is quite unknown to a hidden observer. One of them looks at the other and says—something. What?

It might be: "Joe! How are you?" (Health is a major concern of American culture, but you don't have that clue on Sirius Nine.)

It might be: "Joe! How're the wife and kids?" (Same clue, plus knowledge of the typical family structure. Elsewhere, it might be *wives* and kids or some other permutation.)

It might be: "Hey! You old bastard, molested any kids today?" (Joking relationships are common in America.)

It might also be: "Ah! I've been looking for you. We're late for the conference." (Americans are slaves to clock time.)

It might be nearly anything.

Without even the hints that might be provided by a familiar cultural system, the voices from Sirius Nine were just that—voices. They were sound patterns without meaning. It would definitely not be possible to land on the planet in a blaze of glory, stroll up to the nearest inhabitant, and say, "Greetings, O Man-Who-Is-My-Brother! I come from beyond the sky, wallowing in good will, to bring you all the jazzy benefits of civilization. Come, let us go arm in arm to the jolly old Council of the Wise Ones. . . ."

"I'm going nuts," Charlie said. "Got any suggestions?"

"Just keep digging, that's all. We'll probably have to work out a nonverbal approach, but if you're set up to learn the language in a hurry once you get the chance, that's all we can expect. Anything I can do for you?"

Jenike smiled, showing singularly yellow teeth. "Yeah, you can get out of here and let me work."

Monte stifled a ready reply; he was going to keep things running smoothly if it killed him. "See you around, then."

He started to duck out through the door.

"Monte?"

"Yep?"

"Don't mind me. Thanks for coming by."

"Don't mention it."

Feeling a little better, he closed the door behind him.

The door was not soundproofed. Almost instantly, the voices started up again. He could hear them faintly in the cold silence of the ship: laughing, solemn, playful, querulous.

He started gingerly along the catwalk, and the strange whispers followed him, filling his mind.

Sounds from another world . . .

Voices.

The large, somewhat egg-shaped off-duty room was supplied with tolerably comfortable chairs and grip-top tables. It had a bar of sorts, and the cool air was warmed a

bit by the fog of smoke and voices that tended to character-
ize such watering holes.

There were two distinct groups in the room. Members
of the crew formed a close, noisy circle around the bar. The
anthropologists had marked out their own territory: they
were in conference at one of the corner tables. Monte had
no doubt that the crew thought they were just as alien as
anything likely to be found on Sirius Nine, and there were
times when he agreed with them.

"Garbage, old man," Don King said, crossing his long
legs without disturbing the crease in his trousers. "Absolute
garbage."

Tom Stein blinked his pale blue eyes behind his thick
glasses and pointed a skinny finger at the archeologist. "It's
all just too simple for you. You've poked around with
projectile points and potsherds so long that you think that's
all mankind is. I say it's a mistake to regard those people as
simple until you know for sure what you are talking about."

Don finished off his drink with one long, meticulous
swallow. "You're making problems where there aren't any,
just like old Monte here. Dammit, man, there *are* constants
in culture. We're long past the stage where you can seriously
suggest that a culture is just a crazy collection of unrelated
traits—a thing of shreds and patches, to use Lowie's unhappy phrase. Cultures, as you guys are always insisting, are
hooked together internally. A simple technology, and we
don't even know whether or not they've *got* any technology
on Sirius Nine; I ain't seen any evidence of it yet—*means* a
low level of culture. You don't invent algebra while you're
out digging up roots, my friend. We're dealing with a rudi-
mentary band of hunters and gatherers. Why make them
more complicated than they are?"

Monte puffed on his pipe, enjoying himself. "That's what I'm worried about. How complicated *are* they?"

"For that matter," Janice Stein said, "what *is* a low level of culture? How do you measure it? Who does the evaluating?"

Don ignored the bait and shifted his ground, which was a favorite stunt of his. "It's complicated enough in one sense, I'll tell you that. It may have sounded nice and easy to Heidelman back at the U.N., but what does he know about it? Did you read that official directive we're supposed to be working under? It says we're to make contact with the natives of Sirius Nine. That's a laugh. How in the devil do you 'contact' a world like Sirius Nine? A world is a helluva big place. You'd think they would have found that out back at the U.N."

Ralph Gottschalk moved his big body on his chair. He had a surprisingly soft voice, but everyone listened to him. "I think Don's got a point there. So far as we know, there is no hypothetical uniform culture on Sirius Nine; there are thousands of isolated local groups of food gatherers. If a starship had landed among the San Bushmen of Africa ten thousand years ago, could it then make contact with *Earth*? It seems improbable."

"Why go back ten thousand years?" Louise asked. "If a ship landed on Earth right now, what would happen? Who speaks for all of us?"

Monte shrugged. "We all know that we'll be doing well to make contact with just one group; Heidelman knows that too. But we still have to be careful. A lot depends on what we do on Sirius Nine."

Don King raised his eyebrows. "Why ?"

Monte, who would have asked precisely the same question if he hadn't been in charge of the expedition, took a stab at it. "Apart from the admitted possibility that we may be biting off more than we can chew, it might be argued that we have made at least *some* progress in ethics and law since the time of Cortes and the rest of his merry crew. We can't just sail into a new harbor, run up a flag, and line up at the hog trough."

"I wonder," Don said. "Maybe I'm just cynical because I'm between mates at the moment, but I doubt that line of reasoning very much. We say we're civilized and we carry weapons only to protect ourselves. Sure. We've got enough surplus to afford luxuries like high-minded philosophies. But if things get tough I'll bet we'll be right back where we started from quicker than you can say Cuthbert Pomeroy Gundelfinger; it'll be an eye for an eye, a tooth for a tooth, and a pancreas for a pancreas. If we can't hack it, the military will take over."

"We'd better hack it then," Monte said quietly.

Ralph Gottschalk stood up, looking more than ever like a gorilla. "I'm going back to work, folks."

Monte joined him, leaving the others to their interminable arguments.

Together, the two men walked through the cold metal ship to study the reports of the first expedition again.

When Monte came into their rather drab quarters after his umpteenth conference with Admiral York concerning procedures to be followed on Sirius Nine, he found Louise curled up in bed reading a novel. The book was entitled *Lunar Flame,* and Monte recognized it as a more or less current best-seller that—to quote the cover blurb—"ripped the plastalloy lid off the seething passions that boiled inside the Moon Colony."

"Doing a little research?"

Louise slithered around in her provocative silk night-gown, which she wore from time to time for their mutual enjoyment, and grinned at him. "Let's go to the Moon, dear. That's where the real action is."

He sat down on the bed. "I thought you'd be down at the hydroponics tanks."

"I spent an hour there," she said, brushing back her long, uncoiled black hair. "But it's too *chemical*, even for me. Dammit, Monte, I miss our roses. Stupid, isn't it?"

"I don't think so, Lise." He took her in his arms and nudged her cheek with his beard. Her perfume was sensa-tional, which was a not-so-subtle signal. "Three years is a big chunk out of anyone's life. It's funny, the things you miss out here."

"I know. I catch myself thinking about those picnics of ours up in the mountains. Remember that time on Beaver Creek, when you caught all those rainbows and the storm came up? I think the worst thing about a spaceship is that there's no *weather*.'"

"It's not all fun and games," Monte admitted.

Louise changed the subject. "What did Master York have to say?"

Monte hesitated. "Nothing much. He's a very level-headed guy, I think. We were working out the details of res-cue operations—just in case."

Quite suddenly, they became sharply aware of the cold metal of the ship around them, the thin icy sweat, and the great emptiness Outside. . . .

Monte thought of the children they had never had—

Louise had lost two babies in childbirth—and he knew that Louise was thinking of them too. It was a shared sadness between them. They had been planning to adopt a child, but somehow it had never happened.

Louise held him tightly. "You're all I have, Monte. All that counts."

"It works both ways, Lise."

He kissed her, and she kissed him back, and the ritual between them began again.

It always comes back to this, he thought. *After all the small triumphs and major sorrows that make up a life, it comes back to the two of us alone in a room. Without her, my universe has no meaning.*

And then: *Monte, you're a sentimental slob.*

And then: *What the hell! I like it this way!*

"And so do I," Louise whispered, reading his mind with the ease of long practice.

In the darkness of the artificial night, with Louise asleep by his side, Monte Stewart woke up. He had been dreaming, and the dream had not been pleasant. He felt a chill in his bones.

He lay quite still, his eyes open, staring into blackness.

Maybe it's the ship that gives me the jitters. Maybe it's the cold dead air that sighs from the vents, or the vibration of the stardrive, or the gravity that's never quite right. Maybe it's the gray metal coffin that seals me in. . . .

No.

Come off of it, Monte.

You know what it is.

Sure, he knew. The alien forms of life that had been found in the Centaurus and Procyon systems hadn't worried him. They were *really* alien, so utterly different from human beings that there was no possible point of conflict, any more than there was between a trout and a pine tree. When life-forms are totally different, they can usually manage to ignore one another. But when they are close—well, there was unexpected truth in the old phrase about being too close for comfort.

In a way, Monte felt, they had all been talking around the central problem, pretending that it didn't exist. In the long run, it might not matter much whether or not the people of Sirius Nine had a culture that was more complex than it seemed to be.

The crucial point was simply that they *were* people.

The one animal mankind had to fear was man; so it had always been and might always be.

In one sense, Monte Stewart was going to meet a native of another world.

In another sense, and an equally real one, man was at last going to meet man—his sometime friend and his most ancient enemy.

$$\boxed{4}$$

THERE ARE A number of much-advertised facts, Monte discovered, that a man doesn't give a hoot in Hades about when he's actually *living* on an alien planet. Prominent among them are the following:

The star Sirius is twenty-six times as bright as the Sun of Earth, and two and one-half times as massive. It has a temperature of 19,700 degrees Fahrenheit. It has a white dwarf star for a companion, which revolves around it every fifty years. The dwarf is a long way off—twenty times the distance from the Earth to the Sun—and it is only a little more than three times the width of the Earth. Sirius has twelve planets, and the ninth one, very far out in an elliptical orbit, is similar enough to pass for a cousin, if not a twin, of Earth. The planet has five percent more nitrogen in its atmosphere than does the Earth, and slightly less oxygen.

On the other hand, there were certain facts that a man could not ignore. These were the ones that kicked him in the teeth:

The sun is a blinding white; a raging giant furnace in

the sky. If you are not careful, it blisters your skin with disconcerting speed. The daylight hours—there are ten of them—are oppressively hot, and the air is humid; your shirt is plastered to your back ten minutes after you put it on. The gravity, particularly after the months on the ship, is a shade too strong and your feet feel as though they have picked up heavy gobs of mud with each step you take. Something in the air doesn't agree with you; your nose itches constantly and your throat is always sore. Strange animals sniff you on the heavy wind and panic at the smell. The rolling grasslands look very pleasant, but they are *never* level—you are always either climbing or descending a deceptive grade, and there is a liberal supply of burrs and thorns to rip at your skin and your clothing. The great forests that grow in bands along the bases of the jagged mountains are gloomy and still, and the reddish leaves of the trees remind you of a nightmare autumn. There are dirty-gray clouds on the horizon, and muted thunder mutters down the wind. . . .

Monte wiped the sweat out of his eyes with his damp sleeve and tried to find a less slippery grip on his rifle. He had been on Sirius Nine for two weeks now, and in his considered opinion had accomplished precisely nothing. He had seen the natives with his own eyes, and knew no more about them than he had known on Earth. Journeying across the light-years, he thought, was sometimes easy when compared to crossing from one man's mind to another's.

For the first time in his life, he genuinely understood that a culture, a way of life, could be a totally alien thing— something for which there was no counterpart on Earth at all. Nothing in his previous experience had prepared him for the reality of the people on Sirius Nine. Now, struggling through the thick grass of the field with Charlie Jenike at his side, he could not forget what he had written the night before in his notebook. (He kept two sets of notebooks, an official one and one for himself. So far, the official one was virtually blank.)

It's frightening to realize how ignorant we are, and how thoroughly conditioned by our own limited experiences. Stories and learned speculations about life on other planets always seem to emphasize the strange and exotic qualities of the alien worlds themselves, but the life-forms that exist against these dramatic backdrops all live like earthmen, no matter how odd their appearance may be. (Or else they live like social insects, which amounts to the same thing.) All the caterpillars and octopi and reptiles and frogs have social systems just like the Vikings or the Kwakiutls or the Zulus. Nobody seems to have realized that a culture too may be alien, more alien than any planet of bubbling lead. You can walk right up to something that looks like a man—and is a man—and not know him at all, or anything about him. . . .

Charlie sneezed. "Kleenex will make a fortune here."

Monte squinted, trying to see over the curtain of grass that surrounded him. "Dammit, I think we've lost him again." He glanced up at the large gray reconnaissance sphere that hovered in the sky above them, then spoke into his wrist radio: "How are we doing, Ace? I can't see a thing down here."

The soft, Texas voice of Ace Reid, who was piloting the sphere, was reassuring. "He's right where he was, sir. Just at the edge of the trees. You're right on target if he doesn't panic."

"Thanks. Stand by." He cut off the radio and concentrated on trying to avoid the hidden thorns in the grass. His throat was sore and his eyes were inflamed. The day was cloudy, fortunately, but the heat was almost unbearably sticky. He felt like the wrath of God, and he was none too optimistic about what he was doing. They had tried twice before to make contact—how he was coming to hate that phrase!—with the natives, and had gotten exactly nowhere.

However, there was a possibility that the two of them approaching on foot might not be overly alarming. And the old man they had scouted had *seemed* to be more curious than the others. . . .

"This," Charlie Jenike said, "is murder."

"Earthman's Burden," Monte muttered. He would have preferred to have Ralph Gottschalk with him today, but he desperately needed the linguist just in case the native actually said something. Anyhow, Charlie was trying to be cordial; it wouldn't hurt him to reciprocate.

He pushed on through the sticky blue grass, talking to fill up the silence. "You know, Charlie, it's been a mighty long time since any anthropologist went in absolutely cold. I mean, even the early boys had some sort of a go-between— administrators, someone who knew someone, *somebody*. I feel like one of those Spaniards who washed ashore and looked up to find a bunch of Indians nobody had ever seen before."

"Give me the Indians every time. They're at least from the same planet we are—one of those Spaniards wound up being a chief, you know." Charlie began to sneeze again.

With startling abruptness, they climbed out of the grass and saw the dark shapes of the trees ahead of them. Monte stopped and surveyed the terrain. He didn't see the man. Of course, they still had a good hundred yards to go. . . .

He cut in the radio. "Ace?"

"A little to your left, and dead ahead."

"Right. Thanks." He switched off the radio. "You ready, Charlie?"

"I haven't been taking this stroll to help my digestion."

Monte took a deep breath of the irritating air and wished irrationally that he could light his pipe. It was out of the question, of course. If there were no tobacco-like plants on Sirius Nine, the native might not take too kindly to the spectacle of a strange man with smoke coming out of his mouth.

The two men walked steadily forward, their rifles at the ready.

"Hold it," Charlie whispered suddenly. "I see him."

The man stood right at the edge of the trees, half hidden by the faint shadows. He did not move at all, but he was looking directly at them.

Monte did not hesitate. "Keep moving. Stay behind me and on my right. Don't use that rifle unless I'm actually attacked, and for God's sake, Charlie, try to look friendly."

Monte walked straight toward the man, keeping his pace steady. His heart hammered in his chest. He was within twenty yards of the man, fifteen. . . .

It was the closest he had ever gotten.

The man stood as though rooted to the spot, his dark eyes wide and staring. His pale copper skin gleamed wetly in the light, and the fuzz of golden hair on his head seemed almost electrically alive. His long arms almost touched the ground. The man was completely naked, with a series of

vertical stripes painted on his chest. The stripes were all ver-
milion.

He carried no weapons of any kind.

Ten yards. . . .

Monte stopped. *Dammit,* he thought, *he is a man.
When you get up this close, there is no doubt at all.* Monte
put his rifle down on the ground and held up his hands to
show that they were empty.

The man took one quick step backward. His dark eyes
blinked. He was quite old, Monte noticed, although his
muscles still seemed firm and supple. He looked frightened,
confused, uncertain. But there was something else in his
face, as though a struggle were raging within him. The dark
sunken eyes were sad, and yet strangely eager. . . .

Don't run away. Just don't run away.

Monte slowly fumbled in his pack. He took out a small
piece of raw meat and a cluster of red berries. He held the
meat in his right hand and the berries in his left. He ex-
tended them toward the man.

The old man looked at the food silently. He wiped the
palms of his hands against the bare skin of his legs.

Monte took a step forward.

The man retreated a single step, standing now almost
behind a tall blue-barked tree.

Monte froze, still holding out the food. He didn't know
what to do. If only he could *talk* to the man. . . .

He bent over and put the berries and the meat on the
ground. The he waved Charlie back and retreated ten paces.
They waited. For a long minute that seemed to stretch into
eternity, the old man did nothing at all.

Then, surprisingly, he whistled—one long whistle, and

one short. It sounded exactly like a whistle used to call a dog.

Nothing happened.

The man repeated the whistle, urgently.

This time he got results. An animal whined back in the trees. There was a sound of padded feet slowly moving over a carpet of dead leaves. The sound came closer. . . .

The animal stepped out into the open and stood beside the man. It was a big beast, and the stink of him filled the air. He stood some four feet high and his coat was a dirty gray. His long muscles rippled under his taut skin. His ears flattened along his sleek head and he growled deep in his throat. He looked at the two strangers and bared his sharp, white teeth.

Monte held his ground. The animal looked more like a wolf than anything else, but he was built for speed. His head was very long, with massive jaws. He was a killer; Monte knew it instinctively. He felt exactly the same way he felt when he looked at a rattlesnake.

The wolf-thing sniffed the air and growled again.

The old man whistled, once.

The animal went down low, his belly almost touching the ground, and inched his way forward. It snarled constantly, its long white teeth bared. It looked at Monte, saliva dripping from its jaws. Its eyes were yellow, yellow. . . .

The wolf-thing paused at the meat, then kept coming.

Monte could feel the sweat dripping down his ribs.

The old man took a step forward, and whistled again, angrily. The beast paused reluctantly, still snarling. Then it turned, snatched up the meat, and trotted back to the man by the tree. The man patted its sleek head and nodded, and the wolf-thing disappeared into the forest, taking the meat with him. He held it gingerly in his mouth, not eating it.

Very slowly, the man stepped out and scooped up the berries with his right hand. He stared at Monte, his dark eyes fearful.

Monte took a deep breath. It was now or never. He pointed to himself. "Monte," he said distinctly. He pointed to Charlie. "Charlie," he said.

The man stood there with the berries in his hand. He made no response. His eyes began to shift from point to point, not looking at either of them directly. He seemed very tense and nervous. Once, he glanced up at the gray sphere hovering in the sky.

Monte tried again. He pointed to himself and repeated his name.

The man understood; Monte was certain of that. The dark eyes were quick and intelligent. But he said nothing. He looked like he was trying to make up his mind about something, something terribly important. . . .

Quite suddenly, with no warning at all, the man turned on his heel and walked into the forest. In seconds, he had disappeared from view.

"Wait!" Monte called uselessly. "We won't hurt you, dammit!"

"Try a whistle," Charlie said sarcastically, lowering his rifle.

Monte clenched his fists. Somehow, he felt very much alone now that the man was gone, alone on a world that was a long, long way from home. His skin itched horribly.

He looked up. Great dark clouds filled the sky, and the rumble of thunder sounded closer. He saw a jagged fork of white lightning flicker down into the forest. There was a heavy smell of rain in the air.

Monte made up his mind rapidly. He was *not* going to let that man get away. He called the sphere and dictated a fast report of what had happened. "What's the extent of that forest, Ace?"

"It isn't very wide, sir—not over half a mile. But it stretches out lengthwise a far piece in both directions— maybe two or three miles before it thins out any."

"We're going in after him. I want you to come down low, just above the trees. Let me know at once if he comes out the other side. Keep a fix on us, and if we holler you know what to do."

"You're the boss. But there's a bad storm coming up——"

"I know that. Stand by."

Monte cut off the radio and wiped at his beard with his hand. "He was walking, Charlie. That means there must be a path."

Charlie Jenike eyed the gathering rain clouds without enthusiasm. "What if he takes to the trees?"

"What if he does?" Monte asked impatiently. "Didn't you ever play Tarzan when you were a kid?"

Charlie put his hands on his ample hips and tried to figure out whether or not Monte was seriously considering taking to the trees after the man. He couldn't decide, possibly because Monte himself wasn't sure at this point of what he would or would not do.

Monte picked up his rifle and pushed his way into the forest where the man had vanished. He thought for a moment that he heard the whine of an animal, but that was probably his imagination working. It was hot and breathless among the trees, and the subtly *wrong* shapes of the ferns and bushes gave the whole thing the improbable air of a

make-believe world. The woods were dark with shadows. He
felt cut off, as though he had stepped behind an invisible
wall.

Thunder boomed high above them and the blue-black
limbs of the tall trees stirred fitfully.

"Look there," he said. "There is a path,"

It was just a narrow, twisting trail through the forest. In
one place, where the leaves had been scraped away, there
was a fresh print—the mark of a naked man-like foot, with
the big toe sticking out at an angle like a human thumb.
The path looked like a trail through the woods back home;
there was nothing sinister about it.

But it was too still. Even the birds were silent at their
approach, and no animal stirred.

Monte thought of nothing at all and started down the
path.

The storm hit with a cold wet fist before they had gone
two hundred yards.

A wall of wind smashed through the trees and a roar of
metallic thunder exploded in the invisible sky. Great gray
sheets of wind-driven rain pelted the trees and overflowed
into silver waterfalls that drenched the forest floor.

Monte put his head down and kept going. He heard
Charlie swearing steadily behind him.

The rain was cool and oddly refreshing on his damp
back, and the storm seemed to clear the air in a way that was
surprisingly welcome. In spite of the nerve-jangling bedlam
of sound, he felt better than he had before. His nose stopped
itching and even his sandpapered throat lost some of its
rawness.

He kept a sharp lookout, but it was hard to see anything except the rivers of rain and the dripping bushes and the water-blackened trunks of the trees. The crashing thunder was so continuous that it was impossible to talk. Far above him, the branches of the trees swayed and moaned in the wind.

He was soaked to the skin, but it didn't matter. He shoved his streaming hair out of his eyes and kept on walking. He concentrated just on putting one foot before the other, feeling his feet squishing inside his boots, and he kept looking, looking. . . .

There was still light, but it was a gray and cheerless light that was almost as heavy as the rain. It was a ghost light, fugitive from a hidden sun, and it had the feel of imminent darkness in it. . . .

There.

A tremendous tree to the right of the trail, a tree that looked curiously like a California redwood, a tree that had a black opening in it like a cave. . . .

And a frightened copper face staring out of the hollowness within; two dark eyes peering into the rain.

Monte held up his hand. "There he is!" he hollered.

Charlie came up beside him, his pudgy features almost obscured by countless trickles and rivulets of rain. "Let's grab him and run for it. We can make friends later where it's dry."

Monte smiled and shook his head. It might come to that eventually, but it would be a singularly poor beginning. He stood there with the storm howling around him and desperately tried to come up with something—anything—that would get across the idea that he meant no harm.

He had never before felt quite so keenly the absolute necessity for language. He was hardly closer to the man in the tree than if he had stayed on Earth.

Oh, Charlie had worked out a few phrases in one of the native languages and he *thought* he knew approximately what they meant. But none of the phrases—even assuming that they were correct—went with the situation. It wasn't the fault of the first expedition; they had planted their mikes and cameras well. It was simply the fact that you just don't *say* the right things in casual everyday conversations. A man can go through a lot of days without ever saying, "I am a friend." He can go through several lifetimes very nicely without ever saying something as useful as: "I am a man from another planet, and I only want to talk to you."

The closest thing they had was a sentence that Charlie thought meant something like, "I see that you are awake, and now it is time to eat."

That didn't seem too wildly promising.

"Why doesn't he ask us in?" Charlie hollered. "He's looking right at us."

"I don't need any engraved invitation. Let's barge on in and see what happens."

Monte stepped toward the tree.

The old man looked out at him with dark, staring eyes. Those eyes, Monte thought, reflected a lifetime of experiences, and *all* of those experiences were alien to a man from Earth. The man seemed somehow to be of another time as well as another world; a creature of the forests, shy and afraid, ready to panic. . . .

"Charlie! Give it a try!"

Charlie Jenike cupped his hands around his mouth and bellowed a strange series of sounds; it sounded a bit like singing, although his voice was distinctly unmusical. "I see that you are awake," he hoped he said in the native tongue, "and now it is time to eat!"

The old man shrank back into the hollow of the tree, his mouth falling open in astonishment.

Monte took another step closer.

Instantly, without any warning, the man bolted.

He lunged out of his shelter, very fast despite his age, and ran awkwardly, his long arms pumping the air. He came so close that Monte actually touched him as he passed. He scrambled up a tree with amazing agility, wrapping his arms around the trunk and pushing with his feet on the wet bark. When he got up to where the limbs were strong, he threw one questioning glance back down at the two strangers and then leaped gracefully from one limb to another. He used his hands almost like hooks, swinging his body on his long arms in breath-taking arcs. The rain didn't seem to bother him at all; he moved so fast that he was practically a blur.

In seconds, he was gone—lost on the roof of the world.

"Well, Tarzan?"

Monte stood there in the pouring rain. He was beginning to get a trifle impatient with this interminable game of hide-and-seek.

"I'm going inside," he said, taking out his pocket flashlight.

Charlie eyed the dark cave in the hollow tree. "That thing may not be empty, you know."

"I hope it isn't."

"After you, my friend—and watch out for Rover."

Monte walked steadily over to the opening in the tree and stepped inside.

5

THERE WAS A heavy animal smell inside the chamber in the hollow tree, but Monte knew at once that the place was empty. He flashed the light around to make certain, but his eyes only confirmed the evidence of an older, subtler sense. The room—if that was the word for it—felt empty and was empty.

In fact, it was the *emptiest* place Monte had ever seen.

He moved on in, making room for Charlie, and the two men stood there in the welcome dryness, trying to understand what they saw—and what they didn't see.

The interior of the trunk of the great tree was hollow, forming a dry chamber some twelve feet in diameter. About ten feet above their heads, smooth wood plugged the tubular shaft, forming a ceiling that reflected their lights.

The place was a featureless vault made entirely from the living wood of the tree. Even the floor was wood—a worn, brownish wood that was porous enough so that the water that dripped from their clothes seeped away before it had a chance to collect in puddles. The curving walls were a lighter color, almost that of yellow pine, and they were spotlessly clean.

There was a kind of shelf set into one wall; it was little more than an indentation in the wood. The piece of raw meat that the wolf-thing had taken was on the shelf, and so was the cluster of berries.

That was all.

There was no furniture of any kind. There were no beds, no chairs, no tables. They were no decorations on the walls, no art-work of any sort. There were no tools, no weapons. There were no pots, no bowls, no baskets.

The place was absolutely barren. There were no clues as to what sort of a man might live there.

It was just a big hole in a tree: simple, crude, unimpressive.

And yet. . . .

Monte looked closely at the walls. "No sign of chopping or cutting."

"No. It's smooth as glass. No trace of charring, either."

"How the devil did he make this place?"

"Like Topsy," Charlie said, "it just growed."

Monte shook his head. "I doubt that. I never saw a hollow tree that looked like this on the inside, did you?"

"Nope—but then I haven't been in just a whole hell of a lot of them."

Outside, the rain poured down around the tree and the wind moaned through a faraway sky. It was not unpleasant to be in the hollow tree; there was something secure and enduring about the place, as though it had weathered many seasons and many storms.

But how could a man have lived here and left so few traces of his existence?

"Maybe he doesn't live here," Monte said slowly. "Maybe this is just a sort of temporary camp—a shelter of some kind."

Charlie shrugged. There were dark circles around his eyes and he looked very tired. "I'd say that these people have no material culture at all—and that, my friend, doesn't make sense. You know what this place looks like? It looks like an animal den."

"It would—but it feels wrong. Too clean, for one thing. No bones, no debris of any kind. And I'm not at all sure that this is a natural tree."

"Supernatural, maybe?"

"I mean I think it has been *shaped* somehow."

Charlie sighed. "If they can make a tree grow the way they want it to, why can't they chip out a hunk of flint? It's crazy. This place gives me the creeps, Monte. Let's get out of here before we poke our noses into something we really can't handle."

Monte thought it over. It seemed obvious that the man would not return while they were in the tree. Nothing would be gained by parking here indefinitely. But he didn't like the idea of just pulling out. He was beginning to feel a trifle futile, and it was a new experience for him. He didn't like it.

He reached into his pack and took out a good steel knife. He carried it over and placed it on the shelf with the meat and the berries.

"Do you think that's wise?"

Monte rubbed at his beard, which was beginning to itch again. "I don't know. Do you?"

Charlie didn't say anything.

"We've got to do something. And I'd like to see what

that guy will make of a real-for-sure tool. I'm going to get one of the boys in here and plant a scanner and a mike before he comes back. Then maybe we'll see something. I'll take the responsibility."

He cut in his radio and called the sphere. Ace sounded as though he were not exactly having the time of his life bucking the storm above the trees, but he wasn't in any serious trouble. Monte carefully dictated a report of what had happened, and arranged a rendezvous point at the edge of the forest.

"Come on," he said, and stepped back into the rain.

It was quite dark now, and the forest was hushed and gloomy. The rain had settled down into a gentle patter and the thunder seemed lonely and remote, as though it came from another world. They brushed their way through wet leaves and found the trail. The beams of their flashlights were small and lost in the wilderness of night.

Monte walked wearily along the path, his damp clothes sticking to his body. He was bone-tired—not so much from physical exertion, he realized, as from the strain of failure. Still, the night air was fresh and cool after the muggy heat of the day, and that was something.

All forests, he supposed, were pretty much the same at night. He knew that this one, at any rate, was less alien in the darkness. The trees were only trees, flat black shadows that dripped and stirred around him. Occasionally, he could even catch a glimpse of a cloud-streaked sky above him, and once he even saw a star. With only a slight effort of the imagination, he could feel that he was walking through the night-shrouded woods of Earth, perhaps coming home from a fishing trip, and soon he would walk into a village, where lights twinkled along the streets and magic music drifted out of a bar. . . .

He blinked his eyes and shifted the rifle on his shoulder. *Steady boy. You're a helluva long way from Earth.*

It was hard for him to get used to this world. Sirius Nine was just a name, and less than that; it seemed singularly inappropriate. He wondered what the natives called their world. He wished that he knew the *names* of things. A world was terribly alien, incredibly strange, until it was transformed with names. Names had the power of sorcery; they could change the unknown into the known.

Tired as he was, Monte was filled with a hard determination he hadn't known he possessed.

One day, he'd know those names—or die trying.

EXTRACT FROM THE NOTEBOOK OF MONTE STEWART:

This is the fourteenth night I have spent on Sirius Nine. The camp is silent around me, and Louise is already asleep. God knows I'm tired, but I'm wide awake.

All my life I've heard that old one to the effect that when you know the right questions to ask the answers practically hit you in the face. I've even said as much to students in that other life of mine. (Space travel is a great cure for smugness. I feel pretty damned ignorant out here. I wonder if I wasn't getting a mite cocky, back home?)

Well, I think I know some of the right questions. Here are the obvious ones:

What was that man we chased doing in the forest by himself? And, if he lives in that hollow tree, does he

live there alone? Wherever you find him, man is a social
animal—he lives in groups. Families, clans, bands,
tribes, nations—the names don't matter. But a man
alone is a very strange thing. And he isn't the only one,
either; we've seen others. Where is the group he belongs
to? And what kind of a group is it?

What are these people afraid of? The first expedition did nothing to alarm them. Presumably, they have
never seen men like us before—we have given them no
reason to believe that we're dangerous. I'm sure that old
man wanted to talk to us—but he just couldn't make
himself do it. Why not? Most primitive peoples, when
they meet a new kind of men for the first time, either
trot out the gals for a welcome or open up with spears
and arrows. These natives don't do anything at all. Am I
missing something here? Or are they just shy? Or what?

Why don't these people have any artifacts? I
haven't seen a single tool or weapon of any sort. Don
King hasn't been able to find any artifacts in archeo-
logical deposits. What's the answer? Are they so simple
that they don't even know how to chip flint? If so, they
are more technologically primitive than the men who
lived on Earth a million years ago.

Why have they retained the long, ape-like arms of
brachiators? Why do they swing through the trees when
they can walk reasonably well on the ground? Is this
connected in some way with their lack of tools? Are we
really dealing here with a bright bunch of apes? And if
we are, then how about the language? (Question: Is a
bright ape with a language a man? Where do you draw
the line? Or do we have to get metaphysical about it?

And if they are apes, how are we supposed to contact them for the United Nations?)

What's the significance of that wolf-thing we saw? Charlie and I saw the man call Rover with a whistle. We saw Rover pick up the meat and carry it off. Later, we saw the meat inside the hollow tree. (Problem: Was the man going to eat it, or was Rover?) The man certainly seemed to control Rover. So is Rover a domesticated animal, or what? On Earth, man didn't domesticate the dog until after he'd used tools for close to a million years. Are there other animals they have domesticated?

How about the hollow tree? Is it natural, or do the natives shape the growth in some way? If they do, isn't this an artifact? If they can do that, why don't they have agriculture?

Those are some of the right questions.

I'm waiting for the answers to hit me in the face— but I'm not holding my breath.

Two days later, the watched pot began to boil.

First, the old man returned to the hollow tree and found the steel knife.

Then Ralph Gottschalk and Don King spotted a tree burial.

And, finally, Tom Stein—who was cruising around with Ace in the reconnaissance sphere—located an entire village that contained at least one hundred people.

Monte didn't know exactly what he had expected the man to do with the knife; he would hardly have been surprised if he had swallowed it. He and Louise stood by the scanner screen and watched intently as the man entered the hollow tree for the first time since Monte and Charlie had left.

The tree chamber was as Spartan as ever; nothing had changed. The knife was still on the ledge by the meat and the berries. Considering the probable condition of the meat by now, Monte was just as glad that the scanner did not transmit smells.

The old man stood in the center of the room, his dark eyes peering about cautiously in the half-light. His nose wrinkled in a very human way and he picked up the meat and threw it outside. Then he walked back to the shelf and looked at the knife. He stood there for a long time, a naked old man staring at a gift that must have seemed very strange to him, a gift that had been made light-years away.

Then he picked up the knife. He held it awkwardly, between his thumb and forefinger, as a man might hold a dead fish by the tail. He lifted it to his nose and sniffed it. He got a better grip on the handle and gingerly touched the cutting edge with the fingers of his other hand. He muttered something to himself that the mike didn't catch, then frowned.

He walked over to the curving wall and stuck the point of the knife into the wood. He yanked it out again, looked at it, and then shaved a sliver of wood from the wall with the cutting edge. His action left a single raw scar in the polished smoothness of the room.

"Merc kuprai," he said distinctly. It was the first time Monte had ever heard the man speak; his voice was low and pleasant.

"Charlie said that *merc* was a kind of polysynthetic word," he whispered to Louise. "It means something like: *It is a*————. So he's saying that the knife is a *kuprai*, whatever that is."

"Whatever it is," Louise said, "it must not be very impressive."

The naked man shook his head sadly and tossed the knife back up on the shelf. He did not look at it again. He yawned a little, stretched, and walked out of the chamber. The scanner still caught his back, just beyond the entrance to the tree. He sat down in a small patch of sunlight and promptly went to sleep.

"Well, I'll be damned," Monte said.

Louise shrugged, her brown eyes twinkling. "Merc kuprai," she said.

"You, dear, can go to the devil."

She gave him a quick, warm kiss. "You seem to be oriented toward the nether regions today. Look up! Have faith! Remember that every day in every way————"

"Cut it out, Lise," he grinned.

That was when Ralph Gottschalk came lumbering in like an amiable gorilla. His face was flushed and he was smiling from ear to ear. Since Ralph was hardly the type to get excited over nothing, Monte decided that he must have found not only the missing link but quite possibly the whole chain.

"Monte, we've got one!"

"Swell. One what?"

"Confound it, man, a burial! We've got us a skeleton."

The man's excitement was contagious, but Monte held a tight rein on himself. It wouldn't do to go off half-cocked. "Where? You haven't touched it, have you?"

"Of course not! Do I look like a sap? But you've got to

see it! Don and I just found it about an hour ago—it's not a
quarter of a mile from camp. The son of a gun is up in a
tree!"

"Are you sure of what it is?"

"Of course I'm sure—I climbed up and looked. The
bones are in a kind of a nest up there—a regular flexed tree
burial. Man, you ought to see the ulna on that thing! And
I'll tell you this—that mandible may be heavy, but there's
plenty of room for a brain inside that skull. In fact——"

"Anything in that nest except bones?"

"Nothing at all. No pots, no pans, no spears, no nothing. Just bones. But you give me an hour with those bones
where I can really see 'em and I'll be able to tell you something for sure about these people!"

Louise touched his arm. "Come on, Monte! Let's go."

"I'd better have a look," Monte agreed. "Lead the way,
Ralph."

Ralph charged off, still mumbling to himself. He
ploughed through the scattered tents of the camp, crossed
the clearing, and plunged into a stand of trees at an impatient trot. Monte was amazed at the big man's agility; the
tug of the gravity and the enervating effects of the damp
heat did not combine to make a sprint through the forest his
idea of a swell time. Louise seemed to be taking it well
enough, however, so he couldn't afford to say anything
about it.

Don King was waiting for them at the base of a tall tree.
Monte wiped the sweat out of his eyes and was annoyed to
notice that Don looked as natty as ever.

"Hello, Don. Ralph tells me that you two have nosed
out a burial."

Don pointed. "Right up there, boss. See that thing that looks like a nest on that big limb? No—the other side, right close to the tree trunk."

"I see it," Louise said.

Monte examined it as well as he could from where he stood. It looked very much like a nest that might have been made by a large bird, although it seemed to be made mostly of bark. He chewed on his lower lip. If he could just get his hands on those bones. . . .

"Well, Monte? What do you say?"

Monte sighed. "You know what I have to say, Ralph. It's no go. We can't move those bones."

Don King swore under his breath. "It's the first solid lead we've gotten! What's the big idea?"

Monte put his hands on his hips and stuck out his bearded jaw. The accumulated frustrations of this job were beginning to get him on edge. "In case you haven't heard," he said evenly, "we are trying our feeble best to make friends with these people. It would seem to me that desecrating one of their graves would be a fine way of not going about it."

"Oh Lord," Don groaned. "Next you'll be telling me that those bones were probably somebody's mother."

"Not necessarily. They might just be somebody's old man. But I haven't got the slightest doubt that we're being watched all the time. I'd like to have those bones just as much as you would—maybe more. But we're not going to steal them—not yet, anyway. It may come to that. But it hasn't yet. Until I say otherwise, the bones stay there. Understand?"

Don King didn't say anything. He looked disgusted.

"I guess he's right," Ralph said slowly. "Sometimes we have a tendency to forget what those bones mean to people. You remember that joker in Mexico in the old days who tried to buy a body right at the funeral? He almost wound up in a box himself."

"Nuts," Don said.

Even Louise looked disappointed.

"Let's go on back to camp," Monte said, none too happy himself. "Those bones won't run away. They'll still be there when the time is right."

"When will that be?" Don asked, running a hand through his sandy hair.

"I'll let you know," Monte said grimly.

It was indeed fortunate, in view of the general morale, that the reconnaissance sphere landed when it did with the big news. The usually reserved Tom Stein popped out like a jack-in-the-box, just as excited as Ralph had been about the tree burial. His pale blue eyes flashed behind his thick glasses and he even forgot to be analytical.

"Ace and I found a whole bunch of 'em about ten miles north of here," he said. "It must be the main local village or something—at least a hundred of them. They're living in caves. We saw kids and everything. How about that?"

"That's wonderful, Tom," Monte said. "Maybe we can do some good with them. Maybe if we catch a lot of 'em in one place. . . ." He thought for a moment. "Tomorrow we're going to take that recon sphere and set it down right smack in the middle of those caves. We're going to make those people talk if we have to give them the third degree."

"Hey, Janice!" Tom yelled to his wife, "Did you hear what I found? There's a whole bunch of 'em. . . ."

Monte smiled.

Things *were* looking a little better.

An alien yellow moon rode high over the dark screen of the trees and the orange firelight threw leaping black shadows across the flat surfaces of the tents.

Monte, lying on his back on his cot, understood for the first time that the old saying about feeling invisible eyes staring at you was literally true. He knew that the camp was ringed with eyes, eyes that probed and stared and evaluated. It was not a pleasant feeling, but it was the way he had wanted it to be. Indeed, the main reason for establishing the camp in the clearing had been to give the natives a chance to size them up. He hoped they liked what they saw.

Ralph Gottschalk, his back propped up against a stump, was strumming the guitar he had insisted on bringing from Earth. He and Don King—who had a surprisingly good voice—were singing snatches of various old songs: *John Henry*, *When My Blue Moon Turns to Gold Again*, *San Antonio Rose*, *Wabash Cannonball*. As was usually the case, they didn't quite know all the words, which made for a varied if somewhat incomplete repertoire.

It was good to hear the old songs; they were a link with home. And, somehow, the whole scene was oddly reassuring. It was all so familiar, and at the same time so forever new: the dance of the fire, the distant stars, the singing voices. How many men and women had gathered around how many fires to sing how many songs since man was first born? Perhaps, in the final analysis, it was moments like this that were the measure of man; no one, on such a night, could believe that man was wholly evil.

And the natives of Sirius Nine? Did they too have their songs, and of what did they sing?

"It's beautiful," Louise said, sharing his mood as always.

Monte left his cot and went to her. He held her in his arms and kissed her hair. They did not speak; they had said all the words in the long-ago years, and now there was no need for words. Their love was so much a part of their lives that it was a natural, unquestioned power. There was too little love on any world, in any universe. They treasured each other, and were unashamed.

Tomorrow, there would be the caves and the natives and the curious problems of men that filled the daylight hours.

For tonight, there was love—and that was enough.

6

THE GRAY RECONNAISSANCE sphere floated through the sky like a strange metallic bubble in the depths of an alien sea. The white furnace of the sun burned away the morning mists, leaving the vault of the sky clean and blue as though it had been freshly created the night before.

"There it is," Tom Stein said, pointing. "See? They're starting to come out now."

Ace Reid, unbidden, began to take the sphere down.

Far below them, Monte could see a panorama that might have been transmitted from the dawn of time. There was a sun-washed canyon that trenched its way through eroded walls of brown rock, and a stream of silver-streaked water that snaked its way across the canyon floor. Reddish-green brush lined the banks of the stream, and it looked cool and inviting. (Old habits and patterns of thought died hard; Monte caught himself wondering whether or not the fishing was any good down there.) At the head of the canyon, not far from the leaping white spray of a waterfall, there was a jumbled escarpment of gray and brown rock. The face of the rock was pockmarked with the dark cave-eyes of tunnels and rock shelters. There was even a curl of blue smoke rising from the mouth of one of the caves, which was the first real evidence of fire that Monte had seen among the natives.

He could see the people clearly, like toy soldiers deployed in a miniature world. There were men and women in front of the caves and on the steep paths that wound down to the canyon floor. Three or four kids were already down by the stream, splashing in the water. The people must have seen the sphere, which was plainly visible in the blue morning sky, but they didn't seem to be paying any attention to it.

"Look good, Charlie?"

The linguist smiled. "If they'll only *say* something."

Monte turned to Ace. "Set her down."

"Where?"

"Just as close to that cliff as you can get. Try not to squash anybody, but let 'em feel the breeze. I'm a mite tired of being ignored."

Ace grinned. "I'll park this crate right on their outhouse."

The gray sphere started down.

They shaved the canyon walls and landed directly below the cave entrances. Monte unfastened the hatch and climbed out. The brown rock walls of the canyon seemed higher than they had looked from above, rearing up over his head like mountains. The blue sky seemed far away. He could hear the chuckling gurgle of the stream and feel the gentle stir of the wind on his face. He stood there by the metal sphere and the others joined him.

Suddenly, he was almost overpowered by a feeling of strangeness. It wasn't this world that was strange, nor was it the natives who were all around him. It was himself, and it was Tom and Charlie and Ace, with their stubby arms and their layers of clothing. And it was the gray metal sphere they stood beside, a monstrous artificial thing in this valley of stone and water and living plants. . . .

The people did not react to their presence. They seemed to freeze, neither coming closer nor attempting to get away. They just stood where they were, watching.

What was the matter with them? Didn't they have any curiosity at all? Monte began to doubt his own knowledge; he wondered whether all of his training and all of his experience had been any good at all.

Me, the expert on man! I might as well be a caterpillar.

Then, at last, a child moved a little way down the trail from one of the caves. He pointed at the sphere and laughed—a high, delighted giggle. The people began to move again, going on about their business—whatever that may have been. They were so close that Monte could practically reach out and touch them, and yet he felt as though he were watching them from across some stupendous, uncrossable gulf. He simply didn't *get* them, didn't understand what he was seeing. The natives had nothing; they lived in caves and hollow trees. Their activities seemed aimless to him; they didn't seem to do anything that had any purpose to it. They appeared unperturbed, and worse, incurious.

Yet somehow, they did not give him an impression of *primitiveness*. (He recognized that that was a weasel word, but he could only think in terms of the words and concepts he knew.) It was rather that they were remote, detached, alien. They lived in a world that was perceived differently, where things had different values. . . .

An old man, considerably older than the one they had tracked to the hollow tree, walked with difficulty down the trail and stood there just above the sphere. He blinked at them with cloudy eyes and hunched down so that he supported part of his weight on his long arms. The wrinkled skin hung from his face in loose folds, almost like flaps. He was definitely looking at them, not at the sphere. Two young women drifted over and joined him. The child giggled again and nudged one of the wide-eyed girls.

Monte took a deep breath. He felt like a ham actor who had come bouncing out of the wings, waving his straw hat and doing an earnest soft-shoe routine, only to discover belatedly that the theater was empty. . . .

Still, these people did not seem to be afraid. They were not so timid as the man in the tree had been. Perhaps, Monte thought, the people here did share one human attribute: they were braver in bunches.

Monte took a step up toward the old man, who frowned at him and blinked his faded eyes. Monte raised his hands, showing him that they were empty. "Monte," he said, and pointed to himself.

The old man muttered something and stood his ground.

Monte tried again, feeling as though he were caught up in a cyclical nightmare. "Monte," he said.

The old man nodded slowly and pulled at his ear. "Larst," he said distinctly.

By God! He said something!

Charlie whipped out his notebook and recorded the single precious word in phonetic symbols. Monte smiled broadly, trying to look like the answer to an old man's prayers. "Charlie," he said, pointing. "Tom, Ace."

The old man nodded again. "Larst," he repeated. He sighed. Then, incredibly, he began to point to other things: the caves, the stream, the sky, the kids, the women. For each, he gave the native term—slowly, patiently, as though instructing a backward child. His voice was weak and quavering but his words were clear. Monte matched him with English, then eased himself to one side and let Charlie Jenike take over.

Charlie worked fast, determined to grab his opportunity and hold on tight. He tested phrases and sentences, scribbling as fast as his pen would write. He built up a systematic vocabulary, building on the words he had already learned from the tapes. The old man seemed vaguely surprised at his fluency, and patiently went on talking.

Tom Stein maneuvered two of the kids, both boys, down the trail that led to the stream. He took a length of cord from his pocket and made a skillful cat's cradle on his fingers. The boys were intrigued, and watched him closely. Tom went through his whole bag of string tricks—the anthropologist's ace in the hole—and tried his level best to make friends.

Monte was as excited as though he had just tripped over the Rosetta Stone—which, in a manner of speaking, he had. He stuck to the rules of the game; they were all he had to go on. *Begin with the person in authority.* How many times had he told his students that? *Find out what the power structure is, and work from the top down.* Okay. Swell. Only who *was* the person in authority?

Looking around him, he couldn't be sure. It could hardly be Larst, who was close to senility. It certainly wouldn't be one of the children. The women backed away from him whenever he tried to approach—one of them actually blushed—and they didn't seem to be very likely candidates. One difficulty was that many of the natives were not paying any attention to them at all; they simply went on doing whatever they were doing, and he was unable to get any clear impression of how they ranked. It was very hard, he realized, to size up people who wore no clothing; there were no status symbols to give you a clue. Except, perhaps, for the chest stripes. . . .

He compromised by wandering around with his notebook and trying to map the cave village. The people did not hinder him, but he considered it best not to try to enter the caves themselves. He plotted the distribution of the caves and jotted down brief descriptions of the people he found in front of each one. He took some photographs, which didn't seem to bother the natives at all.

But they had made contact!

That was what counted; the rest would follow in time.

His one thought was to get as much done as possible. He lost himself in his work, forgetting everything else.

The great white sun moved across the arc of the sky and the black shadows lengthened on the floor of the brown-walled canyon. . . .

Monte never knew what it was that warned him. It was nothing specific, nothing dramatic. It certainly wasn't a premonition. It was rather a thread of uneasiness that wormed its way into his brain, a subtle wrongness that grew from the very data he collected.

Long afterward, he told himself a thousand times that he should have seen it before he did. He of all people, moving through the cave village with his notebook and camera, should have caught on. But the plain truth was that he was so excited at actually *working* with the natives that he wasn't thinking clearly; his brain was dulled by the flood of impressions pouring into it.

And, of course, there had been no real cause for alarm in the weeks they had spent on Sirius Nine. Somehow, the human mind continues its age-old habit of fooling itself by moronic extrapolation: because there has been peace there will always be peace, or because there has been war there will always be war. . . .

The thing that triggered Monte's brain back into awareness, oddly enough, was not a man—it was an animal. He spotted the creature sitting in front of one of the caves, apparently warming itself in the late afternoon sun. (If you habitually lived in a furnace, he supposed, it took a good bellows to heat you up a little.) Monte snapped a picture of the thing, then studied it carefully from a short distance away. It certainly was not related to Rover, the powerful wolf-like animal they had seen in the forest. In fact, unless he was very much mistaken, the animal was a primitive type of primate.

It was a small creature, no bigger than a large squirrel. It had a hairless tail like a rat, and its rather chunky body was covered with a reddish-brown fur. (It would have been practically invisible in the branches of the forest trees.) Its head, nodding in the sun, was large and flat-faced, with sharply pointed ears like a fox. The animal had perfectly enormous eyes; they were like saucers. When it looked casually at Monte, the animal resembled two huge eyeballs with a body attached.

Many features about the animal were suggestive of

the tarsier. To be sure, the tarsier was nocturnal, and there was no sign that this animal was equipped for hopping. Still, the tarsier was the closest analogy that Monte could find.

It was the first animal that Monte had seen in the cave village and it prodded his thoughts toward the wolf-thing they had encountered in the forest. It was odd, he reflected, that they had encountered nothing like Rover in the village. As a matter of fact, now that he happened to think about it, it was odd too that . . .

He stood up straight, a sudden chill lancing through his body.

That was it. That was what was wrong about this canyon village. That was what had been bothering him, nagging at him. How could it be?

Monte walked as quickly as he dared over to the trail and scrambled down it. He had to fight to keep himself from running. He hurried over to where Charlie and Larst were still yakking at each other. The old man—he looked positively ancient now—was plainly weary, but he was still answering Charlie's questions.

Monte touched the linguist's shoulder. "Charlie."

Charlie didn't even look around. "Not now, dammit."

"Charlie, this is important."

"Go away. Another hour with this guy——"

"Charlie! We may not have another hour."

That did it. Slowly, reluctantly, Charlie Jenike got to his feet, stretched his sore muscles, and turned around. There were shadows under his eyes and his shirt was soaked with sweat. He was controlling his temper with a visible effort.

"Well?"

"Think carefully. Have you seen any men here today?"

Charlie gave a sigh of exasperation. "Are you blind? What do you think I'm talking to, a horse?"

"I mean young men—or even middle-aged men. Have you seen any?"

Charlie shook his head, puzzled now. "No, I don't think I have. But——"

"But nothing. We've been idiots. *There's no one here except women and kids and old men!*"

Charlie's face went white. "You don't think——"

Monte didn't waste any more time. "Ace," he snapped. "Walk over and get inside the sphere. Call the camp at once. Hurry, man!"

While Ace started for the sphere, Monte eased his way over to where Tom was holding a group of kids enthralled with his string games. He squatted down beside him. "Tom. Try not to look alarmed, but I think we're in trouble. There's not a single solitary man of fighting age in this village. Ace is calling the camp now."

Tom stared at him, the cord forgotten in his hands. "Janice," he whispered. "She's back there——"

Ace stuck his head out of the sphere and hollered: "I'm sorry, sir. The camp doesn't answer."

The three men forgot field technique, forgot everything. As one man, they sprinted for the sphere.

As he ran, Monte's brain shouted at him with a single word, repeated over and over again.

Fool, fool, fool!

Ace had the sphere airborne almost before they were all inside.

They flew at top speed into the gathering shadows of a night that was suddenly dark with menace.

7

THERE WAS NO fire; that was the first thing that Monte
noticed. The camp clearing was gray and still in the
early starlight. Nothing moved. The place was as lifeless as
some forgotten jungle ruin, and the tents—there was something wrong with the tents. . . .

Monte kept his voice steady. "Circle the camp, Ace.
Let's have the lights now."

The sphere went down low and hovered in a slow circle.
The battery of landing lights flashed on.

"Oh God," Tom Stein whispered. "Oh God."

Monte felt his stomach wrench itself into a tight knot.
His mouth opened but no sounds came out. His hands
began to tremble violently.

The tents were ripped to pieces; they were little more
than sagging frames. The clearing was littered with debris—pots and pans and clothing and chairs and bright cans
of food. And there were crumpled, motionless heaps on the
ground. They were very dark and very still.

Monte was a man of his time; he had no experience

with the sort of thing that had happened down below. But he knew a massacre when he saw one. *Slaughter.* That was the word. A word out of the past, a word that was no part of life as he had known it.

He wanted to be sick, but there was no time for that. "Land," he snapped. "Get your rifles ready."

The sphere dropped like a stone and hit the ground with a dull thud. Ace switched on the overhead lights and grabbed a revolver. The men scrambled out through the hatch.

There was an ugly smell in the warm air. Everything was utterly still, utterly lifeless. It seemed that nothing was moving in all the world.

The men advanced in a tight group, hardly breathing. The first body they saw was one of the wolf-things. His dirty-gray coat was black with blood. His white fangs were bared, snarling even in death, and his yellow eyes were open and staring. Monte shoved at the body with his boot; the muscles were already stiff, though not completely so.

The next body was also one of the beasts. His head had almost been blown off.

The third body, lying on its face, was Helen Jenike. Her back was clawed to shreds. Her fingernails were dug into the ground, as though she had tried to seek shelter in a hole. Charlie rolled her over and caught her up in his arms. He began to sob—dry, terrible, wrenching sobs that were torn from the depths of his soul. Monte stared at her face. Helen had always been such a dainty person; this was the first time he had ever seen her with her lipstick smeared and her hair in her eyes. . . .

Monte and Tom and Ace went on. They found Ralph Gottschalk—or what was left of him—surrounded by four of the dead wolf-things. Ralph—big, gentle, Ralph—still had his rifle in his hands. His bloody face was frozen into an expression of incredible hate and fury. One of the wolf-things still had its teeth fastened in his mangled leg. Monte forced the jaws apart and kicked the thing aside.

They went on, across the scattered logs of the dead fire, toward the tents.

The last body they found was Louise.

She lay in the dirt, a red-stained kitchen knife in her hand. She seemed smaller than Monte remembered— a tiny, crumpled, fragile thing. He had never seen her so still. He picked her up and stroked her black hair. He didn't even see the blood. He stood there with his wife in his arms and listened to Charlie sobbing from across the clearing. She seemed so light; she didn't weigh anything at all.

He remembered: it had been a long time ago, on another world. She had turned her ankle in the Colorado mountains and he had carried her to the copter. "God," he had said, "you weigh a ton!" And she had laughed—she had always been laughing, always happy—and she had said, "You're getting old, Monte!"

Old? He was old now.

He sat down on the ground, still holding her. He couldn't think. Somebody's hand was on his shoulder. Ace's. He was dimly grateful, grateful for some small touch of warmth in a world that was cold, cold beyond belief. He shivered and wished vaguely that the fire was going. Louise had liked the fire.

"She's gone! She's not here!"

A voice. Stupid. Who wasn't here? She was here. . . .

Tom Stein, pacing around like a crazy man. Why didn't he sit down? What was the matter with the man?

"Monte! Janice isn't here! She may still be alive."

Slowly, with a dreadful effort, Monte pulled himself back to awareness. It was as though he were far underwater, pulling for the light above him. But there was no light, there was no feeling. There was nothing.

"Monte, we've got to find her!"

He put Louise down, gently. He stood up, his face pasty white, his eyes wild. He looked around. The world was still there.

"Who else is missing?"

"Don isn't here. They may have gotten away. We've got to find her!"

"Yes. We've got to find her." He turned to Ace. "Call the ship. Tell them to stand by for boarding. Tom. Take your rifle and start firing into the air. One shot every ten seconds. Maybe they'll hear you."

Desperate to be doing something, Tom ran off and recovered the rifle he had dropped. He fired. The shot was small and lonely in the darkness.

Monte walked slowly over to Charlie Jenike.

"Let's build a fire. It's cold."

Charlie looked up at him with unseeing eyes.

"Come on, Charlie."

Charlie got to his feet, stricken and lost. He nodded wordlessly.

Together—closer in their grief than they had ever been in a happier world—they began to build a fire.

At the edge of the clearing, Tom Stein fired his rifle at
the sky, once every ten seconds.

There was no warning at all that Don and Janice were
near; they simply materialized out of the forest like two
shadows. Tom almost shot his own wife before he recognized her.

"Why didn't you holler?" he asked fretfully. "Why
didn't you shoot and let me know you were alive?" Then she
was in his arms, clutching him as though she were drowning
and only he could save her. "You're alive," Tom said over
and over again. "You've alive. Are you hurt? You're alive!"
He was so overwhelmed that he didn't even think of thank-
ing Don King for saving her life.

Don was a far cry from the neat, handsome man he had
been a few long hours before. His clothes were torn and his
sandy hair was black with dirt. He was still bleeding from a
gash in his left shoulder. He was trembling with the reaction
to the ordeal he had been through, but he was probably the
calmest man in the clearing. For him, the shock was over.

He sat down before the fire, his head in his hands. He
didn't look at Monte or at Charlie. He said quietly, "I'm
sorry. Sorry as hell. I did the best I could. They were already
dead when I grabbed Janice and lit out."

Monte squatted down beside him. "Nobody's blaming
you. We're just glad you're alive. What happened, Don?"

Don still did not look at them. He stared into the fire
and talked flatly, as though he were describing something
that had happened to someone else a long time ago. "It was
still light, about the middle of the afternoon. We weren't

doing much of anything, just waiting for you to get back. Ralph and I were kidding around about going back to that tree burial and poking into it a little. We didn't do it, though—we were afraid we might offend the little tin gods." He spat into the fire. "All of a sudden a pack of those damned dogs or whatever they are came busting out of the woods. They were on us before we knew what was going on. It was crazy, a nightmare. It all happened so fast we couldn't put up any kind of a defense. They seemed to be going after the women; I don't know why. They snarled all the time, like they had gone mad. I saw some of the native men in the trees. They didn't do anything—jsut watched. They never tried to help—I got the impression they had sent the dogs, but that doesn't make sense. We got our guns and did what we could—Ralph went after one of them with his bare hands. There were too damned many of them. I shot two of them that were after Janice and Ralph hollered at me to run. I couldn't see anything clearly, it was all chaos. I grabbed her and took off into the woods. I didn't know what to do, where to go. Those bastards in the trees could see me, and they could climb better than I could. I knew those dogs could trail us on the ground, and we'd never have a chance. I remembered that tree burial—I guess it was because Ralph and I had just been talking about it—and I headed for that. It turned out to be a good idea, but I don't take any credit for it—we were lucky. We climbed up to that damned nest and just sat there. The natives were all around us for a while, but they didn't do anything—maybe the place is sacred or something. The dogs followed us and I shot a pile of them—ten or twelve, at least. Then I ran out of ammunition; there hadn't been time to grab any spare clips. After a while the dogs went away, and so did the natives. When we heard you shooting we climbed down and came back. That's all. My God, what happened over at that village? Did you guys rape the chief's daughter or something?"

"Nothing happened. Nothing at all."

Charlie Jenike just shook hs head; words were too much trouble.

Monte stood up, keeping his eyes averted from Louise's body. "You get the ship, Ace?"

"Yes, sir. They're standing by. Admiral York is about to blow a fuse. He says for you——"

"The hell with Admiral York. Look, Ace—this will take two trips, understand? Janice goes first; we've got to get her out of here. Tom will go with her, of course. And Don."

"I'll wait for you," Don said.

Monte ignored him. "When you get them stashed away, come and get us. Charlie and I will get the bodies ready—we'll use tent flaps to wrap them in. Take your time, Ace—there's no rush getting back here."

Ace hesitated. "They may come back again, Monte."

"Yes. I hope they do"

Ace looked at him and then headed for the sphere, rounding up the others as he went. The sphere lifted soundlessly into the starlit sky, and was gone.

Monte and Charlie sat by the fire, their rifles in their hands, alone with the dead. The night was utterly silent around them. It was not cold, but both men were shivering.

"Well, Charlie?"

"Yes. Let's get it over with."

They got to their feet and cut up what was left of the tents. Then they did what had to be done.

By unspoken assent, they took care of Ralph first, together.

Then each man did what he could for his wife.

When it was over, they built up the fire again. The damp wood hissed and sputtered, but the flames finally took hold and twisted up toward the sky in hot orange columns. Monte honestly didn't know whether the fire was to keep something away or to lure something in. He was sure that Charlie didn't know either.

Monte sat with his back to the fire, watching the black line of the trees. His vision seemed preternaturally sharp: he could trace the webbing of the branches against the stars. And his hearing was keener than it should have been: he heard each tiny stir of the leaves, every scrape of an insect across the forest floor, each distant night-cry of an invisible bird. He was aware, of course, of the fact that sensory impressions are sometimes heightened at moments of crisis— but that datum was stored in a part of his mind that was not really functioning. He was surprised at his acute awareness, and that was all.

"Why did they do it, Monte? What did we do to them?" Charlie's voice was hoarse and ugly.

"I don't know. I thought we were very careful. Hell, maybe there *wasn't* any reason."

"There's always a reason."

"Is there? I'm beginning to wonder."

Charlie didn't say anything more, and the silence was hard to take. It was better to keep the night filled with words. When he didn't talk he began to think, and when he began to think. . . .

"I guess we made the prize stupid blunder of all time," Monte said slowly. "We figured that because we meant them no harm they must necessarily feel the same way about us. We went in among the cannibal tribe with our hymn books and they popped us in the stewpot. We should have been more careful."

"They seemed so shy, so frightened. Was all that an act? How could we have known, Monte? *How could we have known?*"

"It won't help them to blame ourselves."

"But I do. God, I just went off and left her sitting here——"

"Cut it out, Charlie," he said harshly. "I can't take that."

The silence came between them again, and this time they did not disturb it. They let the heat of the fire bake into their backs and waited for the sphere to return from the orbiting ship. The night around them was vast and filled with strangeness; it was more lonely than the stars that burned in the sky above them, and more filled with mystery. . . .

They both sensed his presence at the same time.

"Monte?"

"Yes. Over there."

They got to their feet, their rifles in their hands. The light was not good, and at first they didn't *see* anything. But they both knew with absolute certainty that there was a native somewhere in the trees, watching them. They knew that there was just one native, and they knew approximately where he was.

Monte was as calm as ice. He squinted his eyes, waiting.

"There he is," Charlie whispered hoarsely.

Monte saw him now. He was up high, up where the branches began to thin out, up where he was outlined against the stars. A tall man, facing them, his long arms reaching up above his head. . . .

The man seemed detached somehow, aloof and unworried. He was not trying to conceal himself. He was just standing there watching them, as though it were the most natural thing in the world to be doing. . . .

Something in Monte snapped—literally snapped. It was as though a taut wire had been suddenly cut. The hate boiled up in him like searing lava; his lips curled back in a snarl.

He did not think, did not want to think. He let himself go. He was surprised at how easy it was, how steady his hands were, how clearly he could see. He even remembered not to hold his breath.

He lifted the rifle; it was as light as a feather. He got the motionless native in his sights. *Sitting duck.* He squeezed the trigger. The rifle bucked against his shoulder and a tongue of fire licked into the night. He was not aware of any sound. The slug caught the native in the belly. Monte smiled. He had wanted a gut shot.

The man doubled up in the tree, grabbing at himself. Then he fell. It took him a long time. He bounced off one branch, screaming, and hit the ground with a soft thud.

Monte and Charlie ran over to him. He was lying on his back, his long arms wrapped around his belly. His sunken eyes were wide with shock and fear. He tried to say something and a gush of blood bubbled out of his mouth.

Monte started for him, but Charlie pushed him aside. "He's mine," he whispered.

Charlie Jenike finished the man off with his rifle butt, and he took his time doing it.

They left the native where he was and went back to their fire. It was blazing brightly. Neither of them spoke.

When the gray sphere drifted down out of the sky, Ace helped them load the bodies of their dead. It didn't take long.

The sphere lifted again toward the invisible ship high above them in the starlit night. Monte looked down and watched the fire in the clearing until it was lost from view.

Then there was only the great night all around them, the great hollow night and the far cold stars. He closed his eyes. There was a terrible emptiness inside of him, an icy ache that cried out to him of something vanished, something lost. . . .

Something that he had been and something that he could never be again.

8

THE FUNERAL WAS mercifully brief, and even had a certain dignity, but it was still a barbaric thing. Monte sat through it in a daze, his mind wandering. How Louise would have hated it all. . . .

"When I die," she had told him once, back in those sunlit days when death was only a word and they had both known that they would live forever, "I don't want any gloomy songs and weeping relatives. I want to be cremated and I want my ashes to be spread in a flower garden, where they'll do some good. You'll see to it, won't you Monte?"

"Afraid I can't," he had said. "I've already promised you for a sacrifice to the Sun God."

The Sun God.

Sirius?

Sacrifice. . . .

There had been one consolation, he supposed, although that was hardly the word for it. Her body, stretched out in its makeshift box, was in space. It was drifting in the emptiness and the stars. Crazily, he wondered whether she was cold. At least she was not buried in the earth, with damp soil sealing her off forever from the light and the sun.

In time, she might even fall into the sun. A strange sun, to be sure, a white furnace of a sun, but still a sun. She might have liked that. . . .

He could not believe that she was gone. Oh, he didn't try to kid himself about it. She was dead, and his mind accepted the fact. He couldn't console himself with any fuzzy notions that they would meet again in some Great Bye and Bye. But belief is something you feel, not just something your mind cannot reject. Even when he knew that Louise was in a box in space, he found himself listening for her voice, watching for her to come walking through opening doors, wondering why she stayed away now that he needed her so much.

It was unbearable. He shunned the room that they had shared, entering it only to try to sleep (Sleep? He had forgotten what sleep was.) He didn't drink much; drinking only made it worse. He knew that some men hit the bottle in an effort to forget, but that would never work for him. Alcohol only accentuated what he was already feeling; it had always been that way.

But there were times when he had to go into their room. There were times when he had to lie on their bed, and be alone in the darkness. There were times when he saw her clothes and the books she had been reading. There were times when he could smell her perfume, still lingering in the bare, tiny room.

Then he knew that she was gone from him forever.

Then he knew.

* * *

Admiral William York sat behind his polished desk and looked acutely uncomfortable. He was a tall man, tall and lean, and his gray hair was cropped close to his skull. He seemed to be at attention even when he was sitting down, but he was not an unduly formal man. He had warm brown eyes and a face that easily relaxed into a smile. In fact, Monte thought, he was the perfect officer—even to the slight limp that he had when he walked, a limp that hinted discreetly of past deeds of valor. He was a civilized man, and that didn't make the interview any easier.

Monte was aware of the contrast in their appearances. Monte's clothes didn't fit him the way they should; he had lost a lot of weight and was downright skinny. His beard was ragged and his eyes had dark circles under them. Monte was hard, harder than he had ever been, but he was too hard to be flexible any longer. He didn't bend and snap back. He—broke.

It didn't all show, of course; he was glad of that. He was still Monte Stewart, no matter what he felt like inside. But he felt oddly ill at ease, like a schoolboy summoned before the headmaster. He didn't belong here, in this room, with this man. The hum of the air vents bothered him, and the stale metallic smell of the gray ship. The air seemed cold and dead after the warm irritating atmosphere of Sirius Nine; he always seemed to be cold now. . . .

"Drink, Monte?"

"Thank you."

Admiral York poured out a shot of whiskey for each of them. He sipped his, but Monte tossed it down like medicine. York made quite a thing out of lighting a cigarette, doing his best to make Monte relax. Monte didn't want to disappoint him, so he fished out his pipe and began puffing on it. The smoke *did* taste good. That, at least, had not changed.

Admiral York fingered a stapled pile of typewritten pages on his desk. There were fourteen pages, Monte knew, with his signature on the last one.

"Well, Monte?"

"You've read it. It's all there. There isn't anything else to say."

York leaned back in his chair, staring at his cigarette as though it were the most interesting thing in the world. "You realize, of course, that the safety of this expedition is my responsibility. I have to take most of the blame for what happened down there."

Monte sighed. "You're not a fool, Bill, so don't act like one. I made all the decisions with the natives. I was careful to make that clear in my report, in case there should be any question about it later. It wasn't your fault."

"Perhaps. But it *will* be if anything else happens, so nothing else is going to happen. We know what we're up against now."

"Do we? I wish you'd let me in on it."

"You know what I mean."

"That's what you keep telling me. But I *don't.*"

York shrugged. "Look, Monte, I'm not trying to be difficult. I know that you've had a terrible shock; please believe me when I say that if there were anything I could do to help I would do it."

"I know that, Bill. Sorry."

"The fact remains, however, that I am not a free agent. I have the responsibilities of command here; I must do what I think best."

"And?"

"And I'm taking this ship back to Earth, Monte. I can't risk any further bloodshed. The decisions from now on will have to be made by higher authorities."

"You mean Heidelman?"

"I mean the secretary-general. Surely you realize the situation we've gotten ourselves into here? You do understand, don't you?"

Monte puffed on his pipe. He felt his hands begin to tremble and it made him mad. "You mean that we've failed. That it was all for nothing. That we're just going to turn tail and run."

York looked away. "Isn't that about the size of it? Think, man! You can't go back there. You must be able to see that. It was bad enough the first time. Now the natives have attacked us and killed some of our people. Worse than that, maybe, you've killed one of the natives. I'm not blaming you; I might have done the same. But we've got to draw the line somewhere. We didn't come here to start a war."

"What did we come here for?"

"That's your department, not mine. My job was to get you here and get you back. That's what I intend to do."

"Very fine, very noble. Maybe you'll get a medal out of it, huh?"

"There's no call to get sarcastic. I'm trying to be reasonable with you. You're being bull-headed, not me. It's always easy to blame the brass."

Monte got to his feet, his pipe clamped between his teeth. "Hell, I know I'm taking it out on you." He looked at York with weary eyes. "How do you think I feel? My wife is dead. Ralph is dead. Helen is dead. And I've flopped in the biggest job I ever had. Ever think of yourself as a failure? I never had. I always thought I could do anything. Maybe things came too easy for me; I don't know. I've had my nose rubbed in the dirt, but good. But I'm no quitter. I'm not through yet."

"But what can you *do?* I'm all for this hands-across-space stuff; I believe in it. But it's absurd to sacrifice yourself for the glories of anthropology. You're not thinking straight——"

"To hell with anthropology! What kind of a jerk do you take me for? It's bigger than that and you know it. If we foul it up now there may never be another chance. The next outfit that comes out here—if there is a next outfit—will be a military expedition. Do you want that?"

"No. No, I don't."

"Okay. I loused up the first try. It's up to me to set it straight. It's my job. I want to do it, that's all."

"I can't let you risk the others."

"No, of course not. But who are we risking? There is no threat to the ship—they can't get at you here. Janice must certainly stay here, and I wouldn't want Tom to go back. I don't think Don would go anyhow. I don't know about Charlie—that's up to him. But *I* can go back."

"Alone?"

"Why not? The worst that can happen is that I'll get myself knocked off. What difference will that make?"

"Monte, I admire your guts. But I've seen it happen a thousand times—a man loses his wife and he thinks it's the end of the world. It isn't. You're still young——"

"Creeping crud! I've *got* to go back. I've got to live with myself; Louise or no Louise. Suppose you were sent out on a big assignment and you lost the first skirmish. Would you run for home? Would you?"

York hesitated. "Maybe. If I saw that there was no hope at all——"

"But you don't *know* that! We don't even know what happened down there, not really. We've got enough of the language now so that we can talk to them. We made some progress. Look, you're clear on all this. It's down in black and white that I'm in charge of all relations with the natives. We came out here to stay a year. I want that year. You can't just order me to go home, not when the ship is in no danger at all. That won't help what happened. We've got to try again."

York poured out another drink and handed it over. "Calm down. Just what do you propose to do? Go back down there with your popgun and start blazing away?"

Monte sat down and swallowed his drink at a gulp. "I swear to you that there will be no more killing. Not even in self-defense."

York looked at him and nodded. "I believe that. But where will it get you? You must have some sort of plan."

"I do. I'm going down there and I'm going to win their confidence. I'm going to find out what makes them tick. When I understand them I can deal with them. I'm going to give Heidelman his peaceful contact if it kills me."

"That's not a plan. That's an ultimatum. We can't trust those people—they've proved that. We've got to consider our own security."

Monte smiled. "That sounds pretty familiar, Bill. That's the old, old road that leads to nowhere. I can't trust him. He can't trust me. So wouldn't it be better to drop a big fat bomb on him before he drops one on me? Do you want to start that up all over again? Do you want that to be the history of Earth's first meeting with other men?"

"You gave them every chance to be friendly!" York was a little red in the face; this was a touchy subject. "You bent over backwards. What did it get you? There's no damn sense in it! I can't let you go back down there and get yourself killed. That *is* my responsibility."

Monte grinned; he was feeling better. "I didn't know you cared."

"Cut it out. I'll go this far with you—I'll give you a week. At the end of that time, I want a plan—a real plan. And you'll have to sell me on it, I warn you. I want a plan that gives a reasonable prospect for success. I want a plan that will ensure your safety. I want a plan we can show the boys back home that makes it dead certain that no more natives get hurt, no matter what good excuses we have. I want the works, in writing."

"You don't want much, do you?"

Admiral York permitted himself a smile. "As the man said, you buttered your bread—now lie in it."

Monte stood up and stuck out his hand. York took it.

"You've got yourself a deal, Bill. Thanks. I won't forget it."

"If this backfires, neither one of us will ever forget it. But good luck. And try to get some sleep, will you?"

"Sleep? Who has time for sleep?"

Monte turned and walked out of the room.

He hurried along the metal catwalks with the great ship all around him, feeling more alive than he had felt in a long time. There were plans to be made. He stuck his pipe in his mouth and set out to find Charlie Jenike.

9

H E FOUND CHARLIE JENIKE where he had known he would be: crouched over his notebooks and recording equipment in the cold little box-like room Charlie used for his linguistics lab. Charlie was so wrapped up in his work that he didn't even hear Monte come in.

Monte studied the man, seeing him with fresh eyes. He had never felt really close to Charlie until that fantastic night by the fire in the bloody clearing on Sirius Nine; there had always been a subtle antagonism between them. It was probably nothing much; they just rubbed each other the wrong way. And yet, somehow, he had been fated to commit a murder with Charlie Jenike. In a universe where strangeness lurked behind every commonplace facade, this was surely one of the strangest things of all.

(Oh yes, it had been murder when they had killed the native. Monte knew it and Charlie knew it. They had not even recognized the man. They had never seen him before. They hadn't known what he wanted or what he was doing. If you come home some night and find your wife has been murdered, you don't just charge out into the street and shoot the first man you find on the principle that one victim is as good as another. Maybe they had been a little crazy, but that didn't excuse them in their own minds. What was it that Don King had said in that bull session so long ago? *"We say we're civilized, which means that we have enough surplus to afford luxuries like high-minded philosophies. But if things got tough I'll bet we'd be right back where we started from quicker than you can say Cuthbert Pomeroy Gundelfinger; it'd be an eye for an eye, a tooth for a tooth, and a pancreas for a pancreas. That's the way men are."* Monte recalled that he had been rather self-righteous in that argument, talking learnedly about progress and ethics and all the rest. He had been pretty sure of himself. But then, it had been a very long time ago. . . .)

Charlie certainly wasn't very impressive physically. He was a dumpy, sloppy man who was losing his nothing-colored hair; if he had ever glanced into the mirror, which was highly unlikely, he would have seen what looked disturbingly like a bulldog's face perched atop a penguin's rotund body. Charlie lacked all of the conventional virtues: he dressed badly, changed his clothes all too infrequently, had little visible charm, and didn't bother to cultivate the civilized buzz of small-talk which serves to cushion our dealings with our fellow seasick passengers on the voyage of life. Nonetheless, Charlie had something, something that was quite rare. Watching him at work, Monte realized that the man had a certain dignity, a certain integrity that had all but vanished from the contemporary scene. The very words *dignity* and *integrity* were slightly suspect these days; like so many others, they had been corrupted by the politicians and the tri-di dramatists. It was a surprising thing to find such a man and to know him—it was something like finding a worm that could do algebra. Now that the chips were down, Monte found that he could turn to Charlie Jenike in a way that he never could with a man like Don King, or even with Tom Stein.

Charlie finally sensed his presence and turned around, his eyebrows lifted questioningly.

"I've been talking to Bill York. He wants to take the ship back to Earth."

"That figures. Will he do it?"

"Unless I can talk him out of it. I'd like to kick it around with you a little, if you don't mind."

The linguist fumbled for a cigarette and lit it. "I'll try to fit you into my list of appointments. Shoot."

Monte filled his pipe and sat down on a hard, straight-backed chair. The whisper of the air vents seemed very loud to him. It was odd that the noise didn't make Charlie's work more difficult than it was. He wondered suddenly why Charlie kept on working as he did. To keep himself from thinking about Helen? Work was a kind of opiate, but that was a feeble explanation. For that matter, Monte didn't know what it was that kept himself working. He smiled a little. He didn't understand Charlie, he didn't understand himself. How could he possibly hope to understand the natives of Sirius Nine?

"How much did you get from Larst?"

"Plenty."

"Enough to talk with them?"

"I think so. I already had a lot of stuff, and the old buzzard gave me enough of a key so that I can work out most of it. It's a curious language—very weak in active verbs. But I can speak it now, after a fashion."

Monte felt a wave of relief. That was one bluff he had pulled with York that had panned out. They had the words, they had a bridge. "What the devil do they call Sirius Nine?"

"That's a tough one. They think of the world in a number of different ways, some of them pretty subjective. They do have a word, though—*Walonka.* It seems to mean a totality of some sort. It means the world, their universe, and it has an idea of unity, of interconnections. It's the closest I can get. They don't quite think in our terms. You know, of course, that it's more than just a matter of finding different labels for the same thing—you have to dig up the conceptual apparatus that they work with. They call themselves *Merdosi,* the People. And they call those damned wolf-things by a very similar term: *Merdosini.* A rough translation would be something like 'Hunters for the People.' Interesting, huh?"

"It makes sense. Did you get anything else suggestive?"

"I got one thing. One of the words that Larst applied to himself has a literal meaning of man-who-is-old-enough-to-stay-in-the-village-all-year-round. What do you make of that?"

Monte frowned. "It must mean that the younger men *don't* stay in the village all the time. And that means—"

"Yeah. When you noticed that none of the younger men were present, you were dead right. But it didn't necessarily mean what we thought it meant—that they were out on a war party of some sort. The attack on our camp might not have been hooked up with their absence at all. Those guys are out in the woods most of the time—maybe they all live in trees like the man we tried to contact."

"But they must come into the village *sometimes.*"

"Obviously. There are kids running around. That would indicate at least occasional proximity."

"You think they have a regular mating season, something like that?"

"I wouldn't know. It's a possibility. But it seems a little far-fetched for such an advanced form of life."

"It wouldn't have to be strictly biological, though. Human beings do funny things sometimes. It might be a situation where there is some slight biological basis—females more receptive at certain times of the year—and then the whole business has gotten tangled up with a mess of cultural taboos. How does that strike you?"

Charlie ground out his cigarette. "Well, it might explain a lot of things. The attack on the camp, for one."

Monte got to his feet, excited now. "By God, that's it! How could we have been so stupid? And to think that I *planned* it that way——"

"You didn't know."

"But I did the worst possible thing! I set up our camp in a clearing, where they could watch us. I wanted them to see what we were like. And we had our women with us, all the time. We *flaunted* them. And then we went to the village with their women——"

"You couldn't have known."

Monte sat down again wearily. "Me, the great anthropologist! Any fool bonehead could have done better. I *should* have known—what was that guy doing in the tree by himself in the first place? We landed and the very first thing we did was to break the strongest taboo in their culture! It was just like they had landed in Chicago or somewhere and had promptly started to mate in the streets. My God!"

"It's something to think about. But that isn't the whole answer."

"No, but it's a lead! They don't seem quite so unfathomable now. Charlie, I *can* crack that culture! I know I can."

Charlie lit another cigarette. "You're going back there." He said it as a simple statement of fact, not as a question.

"Yes. I've got to give York a royal frosted snow-job to do it, but I'm going back."

"Don won't go. York won't let Tom and Janice out of this ship again."

"I don't give a damn. I'm going alone."

"You can forget that. Include me in. I'm going with you."

Monte looked at him. "You don't have to go, Charlie."

"Don't I?"

"You know what the odds are. I don't think we'll ever come back, to tell you the truth."

"So? Who wants to come back? What for?"

Monte sighed. He had no answer for that one.

"We're both crazy. But we've got to come up with a plan for Bill York. An eminently *sane* plan."

"Yeah, sure. Sane."

"Let's hit it. Got any ideas?"

Charlie smiled, relaxing a little. "I've got a few. I was afraid you were going to try to sneak off and leave me here. I was working on a small snow-job of my own."

Monte pulled his chair up to the table and the two men put their heads together.

An hour or so later, a passing crewman was astonished to hear gales of laughter behind the closed door of Charlie Jenike's linguistics lab.

EXTRACT FROM THE NOTEBOOK OF MONTE STEWART:
    I've lost track of time.

    Sure, I know what "day" it is and all that. It's easy to look at the ship's calendar. But it doesn't mean anything to me. (Funny to think of how much trouble a people like the Maya went to in order to invent a calendar more accurate than our own. And even their calendar was forgotten in time; it got to the point where it didn't matter. I wonder why? I wonder what really happened?)

    It seems to me that Louise died only yesterday. That is the only past I know, the only past I have. There is a time when the pain is too much to bear. There is a time when the pain goes away—or so people tell me. Those are the two dates on my calendar.

    I find it almost impossible to work on my official notebook. In this one, the one for myself, I can think. A man can't think in terms of large abstractions like the United Nations and the First Contact with an Alien Culture. It gets to be a personal thing, a personal fight. There comes a time when a man must get up on his own hind legs and admit the truth. I'm doing it for me, for Monte Stewart. I'm doing it because I am what I am.

(And what am I? Cut it out, boy! You're not ready for the giggle academy yet!)

Well, a long time ago I asked myself some questions about the people of Sirius Nine. Or should I say questions about the Merdosi of Walonka? That is progress of a sort. And I think I've got some answers now; the questions must have been good ones. And, as usual, I've got some more questions.

But what do I know?

I know what that man was doing in the forest by himself. The Merdosi have a mating season of some sort. The men live out in the forest most of the time, and only come into the cave village with the gals at certain times of the year. This may be biological, or cultural, or—more probably—both. Question: What in blazes do the men *do* out there in those hollow trees? Question: How do the women and kids get by on their own in the village?

The Merdosi are afraid of us, and I still don't know why. Sure, we broke a powerful taboo by living with our women at the wrong time of the year—but that doesn't explain everything. They attack us because they are afraid of us; I'm certain of that. At other times they try to ignore us. It is as though we are a threat to them simply by being here. Why?

Obviously, there is a very close relationship between the people and the wolf-things—between the Merdosi and the Merdosini. The Merdosini are the Hunters for the People. The two life-forms are interdependent. Can we call this symbiosis? Regardless of the name we tag it with, we have a problem. It's easy to see what the wolf-things do for the natives—they do their hunting for them, and their fighting as well. But what do the natives do for the wolf-things? What do the Merdosini get out of the deal? It must be a very old pattern, but how did it start? How do the natives control those animals? On Earth, the dog probably domes-ticated itself hung around the fire for scraps of food and the like. But that won't work here, because the natives seem to *get* their food—or some of it—from the Merdosini. What's the answer? (And we've got the same puzzle with those tarsier-like critters I saw in the village. Are they just pets, or something else?)

I'm convinced that the key to this whole thing is somehow mixed up with the fact that these people have no tools. We are so used to evaluating people in terms of the artifacts they use that we are lost when these material clues are denied to us. Making tools seems to us to be the very nature of man. The first things we see when we look at a culture are artifacts of some sort: clothes, weapons, boats, skyscrapers, glasses, watches, copters—the works. But most of this culture isn't visible. We can't see it, but it's there.

What can it be like? Is there a richness here that we are just not equipped to see?

And remember that they do have the concept of tools. They even have a word that means an artifact of some sort: *kuprai*. The old man knew what a knife was for, but he was not impressed by it. Well, we have a lot of concepts in our culture that we don't make much use of. I can remember hearing a lot of twaddle about how it doesn't matter whether you win or lose, but only how

you play the game. Try telling that to a football coach.
Try telling that to an honest man whose kids don't have
enough to eat.

Take away all our tools, all the trappings of our civilization, and what do we have left?

What do the Merdosi have?

The gray metallic sphere came down out of cold blackness into warm blue skies. The white inferno of Sirius
burned in the heavens like a baleful eye that looked down
upon a red and steaming world.

The sphere landed in the clearing where the charred
logs told of a fire that once had burned, and bright cans of
food and broken chairs hinted at a meal that had never been
eaten.

The hatch opened and two men climbed out into the
breathless heat of the day. They moved slowly and clumsily,
for their bodies were completely encased in what had been
spacesuits a few days before. They looked like awkward
robots who had somehow strayed into a nightmare jungle in
the beginning of time, and they carried extra heads in their
hands.

Supplies were unloaded and the sphere lifted again into
the wet blue sky and disappeared.

The two men carried no weapons.

They stood for a moment looking at the dark and silent
forest that surrounded them. They heard nothing and saw
nothing. They were not afraid, but they knew that they
faced a world that was no longer indifferent and unprepared.
They faced a world that was totally alien, and a world that
was hostile beyond reason, beyond hope.

They were the Enemy. It was a fact of life.

Strange and unnatural in their stiff-jointed armor, already sweating under the great white furnace of the sun, they methodically began to make camp.

All around them, in the tall trees that reached up to touch the sky, long-armed shadows stirred and watched and waited.

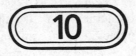

10

MONTE WIPED THE stinging sweat out of his eyes— no simple matter with his hand inside a spacesuit glove—and squinted up at the sun. The swollen white fireball was hanging just above the trees, as though reluctant to set. Its light turned the leaves to flame and sent dark shadow-tongues licking across the clearing.

It had been the longest afternoon of his life. The spacesuits, even with the air vents that had been drilled into them, were miserably hot and clumsy. He felt as though he were standing in twin pools of sweat, and the faint breeze that whispered against his damp face only made the contrast more unbearable. He thought of what it would be like with the helmets on and shuddered.

Still, it was the only way.

His throat was getting sore again from the irritants in the air, but his nose was clear. It was odd, he thought, how different things affected a man at different times on an alien world. Now that he was used to the way Sirius Nine looked, now that he knew that the name of the world was Walonka and its appearance was familiar, he was struck by the way the place *smelled*. Even if he had been blind, he would have known that he was not on Earth.

He smelled the acrid smell of sun-blasted canyons and the brown-rock smell of the mountains. He smelled the bubbling silver of the streams and the close, heavy smell of the trees. He caught the perfume of strange flowers and the greasy scent of vines that crawled up to the roof of the world. He smelled the slow wind that had flowed like oil over places he had never seen. He sniffed the rank odor of furtive animals that padded across the forest floor. He sensed the tang of seasons and woodsmoke and the great vault of the sky, and he smelled things that were unknown and nameless and lost.

How strange it was to smell things that conjured up no memories, brought back no nostalgia. . . .

"Soup's on," Charlie said, looking more grotesque than ever in his bulbous spacesuit. "Get it while it's hot."

"I'll settle for a cold beer."

"Got to eat, don't we? Can't be a hero on an empty stomach, as someone once should have said."

"How about Gandhi? He was good enough to have York's ship named after him."

Charlie tried to shrug, but it was virtually impossible. "He wasn't lugging a spacesuit around on his back. Burns up the old calories, you know."

Monte took a self-heating can that Charlie handed to him and awkwardly spooned out a steaming horror that was supposed to be beef stew. He ate it standing up, for the simple reason that sitting down was too much trouble. He washed the stuff down with a canteen of cold water and was surprised to find that he felt somewhat better.

Sirius was below the rim of the trees now, although it was still flooding the sky with light. There were puffy, moisture-laden clouds on the horizon, and they looked black in the middle and crimson around the edges. It was still hot, but the evening breeze was freshening.

They built up the fire in the clearing until the logs sizzled and popped and white smoke funneled into the sky. They checked their tents and then they were ready.

"Do you see them?" Monte asked.

"No. But I *feel* 'em. They're all around us, up in the trees."

"Time for your speech, wouldn't you say?"

"Are you sure you wouldn't rather do it yourself? You can speak the lingo as well as I can by now."

"Not quite. Anyhow, you're more eloquent. Give 'em the works."

"It's useless, you know."

"Maybe. We've got to try."

Charlie Jenike walked stiff-legged to the other side of the fire. He stood there facing the trees. The fire hissed behind him. He looked somehow more alien than the world he faced: a squat mechanical man that had stepped out of a factory in a dark land beyond the stars.

The red-leafed forest was an abyss of electric silence: waiting, watching, listening.

Charlie Jenike took a deep breath and made his pitch.

"Merdosi!"

There was no answer; Charlie hadn't expected one.

"Merdosi!"

There were only the trees rooted in the hostile soil, only the immense night that rolled in from far away.

"Merdosi! Hear my voice. We do not come to you in anger. We carry no weapons."

(Monte smiled in appreciation; Charlie really *was* good with the native language. That last sentence was a marvel of circumlocution.)

"Merdosi! My people came to Walonka to be friends with your people. We meant you no harm. In our ignorance, we made many mistakes. We are sorry for them. The Merdosi too have made mistakes. It was wrong for you to send the Merdosini after our people. It was wrong to kill. We did not understand, and we too were wrong when we killed one of your men. This clearing has been stained with blood— your blood and our blood. That is past. We want no more killing. We will kill no more. Our only wish is to speak with you in peace."

The shadow-filled forest was silent. A log burned through on the fire and collapsed in a shower of sparks.

Charlie lifted his heavy arm. "Hear me, Merdosi! This is another chance for both of us. We are all people together. We must trust one another. On our world beyond the sky, many bad things have happened because people could not trust each other. Many times the first step was never taken, and that was wrong. Here and now, we are taking the first step. We have come in peace. We have trusted you. We have washed our hands of blood. Come out! Come out and let us sit by the fire and talk as men!"

No voice answered him. In all the darkening hush of the woods, no figure stirred.

"Merdosi! We have learned your words, and we speak them to you. There is nothing to fear! There is much to be gained. Do you not wonder about us, as we wonder about you? Will you not give us a chance, even as we have given you a chance? It is wrong for a man to hide like an animal! Come out! Come out, and let us be men together!"

There was no reply. He might as well have been talking to the trees themselves. Slowly, he let his arm fall to his side. He turned and rejoined Monte by the tents. There was a bleak sadness in his eyes.

"Well," he said, clearing his throat.

"It was good, Charlie. No man could have done any better."

"It wasn't good enough."

"Maybe not. We knew it was a long shot, didn't we? We gave it a try. What the hell."

Monte stroked his matted beard absently. He looked around the little clearing. The firelight seemed brighter now; the long night was near. He found himself looking at the exact spot where Louise had died. Quickly, he averted his eyes.

Charlie snorted. "We're nuts. They're nuts. The whole thing is insane. If we had all our marbles, we'd go back to Earth and forget there ever was a Sirius Nine."

"Think you could forget?"

"Maybe. I could try."

Monte laughed. "I'll tell you, Charlie: it's probably easier for me to come here than it would be to go home, and that's the truth. But the notion is not without its appeal. I could go back to Earth and file a classic report with the U.N. The intrepid anthropologist returns from the stars and gives the boys the word. *The natives are bloodthirsty jerks! I advise that they be obliterated for the good of mankind!* Ought to create quite a stir, hey?"

"Maybe that's just the report you should file," Charlie said soberly.

"There's another good one we could come up with; it would be very popular and would make everybody feel good. *The natives are poor ignorant dopes who don't know what they're doing. I advise that their culture be manipulated by the all-wise earthmen to make them smart like us. I propose an 'earthman's burden' for the good of the universe!* How's that sound?"

"Familiar. Stupid, but familiar."

"The devil of it is that most people would welcome a report like that. It's funny how many people there are who like to play God."

Charlie started to say something, then changed his mind. He walked over and managed to lift another log and toss it on the fire.

"Think we'll last out the night?" he asked casually.

"Maybe."

"Let's get with it. I'd just as soon try to make pals with the Devil as the Merdosi."

"We might have a better chance, at that. After all, the Devil is a product of our own culture a few millenniums back. He's one of the boys, even with his horns and tail. He even speaks our language, according to usually reliable sources. He makes deals."

"To hell with him," Charlie grinned.

"Exactly. Are you ready?"

"Yes."

"Put your helmet on and let me test it."

Charlie picked up his gleaming helmet, stared at it a moment, took a deep breath, and settled it on his shoulders. It clamped into place with an audible click, and Charlie locked the catches with gloved, puffy fingers.

Monte checked the helmet carefully. It was secure. Charlie's face, behind the thick glassite plate, seemed swollen and remote. Monte put on his own helmet and fastened the catches. All sounds from outside ceased. He knew a moment of panic when he felt as though he were smothering, but then the air came in. The doctored suits had breathing holes in the helmets, so that they did not have to depend on canned air.

He spoke into his mike. "All set?" His voice had a hollow sound to his own ears.

Charlie poked at the helmet and gave it a pull or two. "Okay." His voice was tinny in Monte's ears. "You're sealed in like a sardine."

"This ought to be quite a night."

"Yeah. At least we won't die of boredom."

"We may roast to death, though."

"It's a thought."

They fell silent; there was nothing more to say. Monte felt oddly detached, as though his body belonged to someone else. It was already hot in the suit. The silence was overwhelming. The world seemed to have disappeared. . . .

Side by side, like two cumbersome monsters who had lost their way, the two men moved into the sleeping tent. They lowered their heavy bodies onto the protesting cots and lay quietly, their eyes bright behind their glassite plates.

"Now I lay me down to sleep," Charlie said.

Monte said nothing. He stared up into the hushed darkness of the tent and tried not to think.

Outside, the fat yellow moon would be rising. The old, uncaring stars would be looking down on the orange fire that burned in the little clearing. Somewhere, invisibly remote, the ship that had brought him from Earth would be floating in the dark silence.

Sealed in his anachronistic spacesuit, Monte Stewart was as alone as a man could ever be.

He closed his eyes.

Patiently, he waited.

They came out of the night and out of the stillness that lay beneath the silver stars. They came as he had known they would come, on great padded feet, with yellow eyes that gleamed in the close darkness of the tent.

He saw them coming; he was not asleep. They were phantoms, slipping like fog through the entrance to the tent. He could not hear them through his helmet, but he could see their glowing yellow eyes.

He imagined what he could not see: the dirty-gray coat with the long muscles rippling under a taut skin, the long sleek head with the crushing jaws, the saliva dripping from the pulled-back mouth. . . .

He could smell the stink of them, hot and moist and heavy in the trapped air of the tent.

The wolf-things, the killers, the Merdosini.

They had come back to kill again.

"Charlie."

"Yes." The voice was tinny in his ear. "I see them."

He felt nothing, but he could see them nosing at his cot. He could see the black flowing shadows around Charlie's bed.

He lay very still, trying to slow down his breathing. His heart was pounding wildly in his chest. The sweat trickled down from under his arms and it was cold as ice in his hot suit. He waited, not moving a muscle.

Nightmare? Yes, this was what a nightmare was like. A nightmare was all terrible silence and the black shadows of death.

Incredibly, the punch-line of an ancient joke came to him: *Here comes old cold-nose.*

He fought down a mad impulse to laugh, to scream, to yell. These were the beasts that had killed Louise. These were the animals that had destroyed Helen Jenike. These were the killers that had torn Ralph Gottschalk apart.

These were the voiceless horrors of a fevered dream. . . .

The wolf-things attacked.

Suddenly, with mindless ferocity, they were all over him. He couldn't see, couldn't move. The cot must have cracked under their plunging weight, for he felt himself fall to the ground. He was smothered under them, the stink of them filled his nostrils.

He waited, fighting down panic. They couldn't hurt him. He grabbed that thought and held onto it. *They couldn't hurt him.* That was what the spacesuits were for. If your defense is strong enough, you don't have to worry about the offense. The spacesuit was tough and it covered every inch of his body. It would take more than teeth and jaws to tear through that suit. The natives scorned weapons. Very well. Let them try to open a can without a can-opener!

He felt nothing at all, he heard nothing but Charlie breathing into his suit mike. He could not see; one of the things was blocking his face plate. Flat on his back, he tried to move and failed. They must be all over him. . . .

The stench was terrific. He lost track of time. Unbidden, his mind began to work. What if they blocked his air supply? Was the air getting stale? What if they found a fault in the suit, a weak spot, and white teeth began to gnaw at his bones? What if one of the natives came in and unlocked his helmet? What if the natives could direct the wolf-things well enough so that *they* could pry open his helmet, get at his head?

If only he could *see!*

There was some sound coming through the air filters— or was it only his imagination? A wet roaring, a growling, a slavering. . . .

"Charlie!"

"I hear you."

"Can you move?"

"No."

"How long has it been?"

"I don't know."

"What if they don't stop, never stop?"

"You tell me. Calm down, Monte. This is your party, boy."

Monte flushed in hidden shame. Couldn't he take it? What was the matter with him?

If only he could see.

If only he could move. . . .

Suddenly, he *had* to move. He had miscalculated his own staying power; he could not endure this blind suffocation, this being buried alive. He tried to lift his arms and failed. He tried to bend his knees and failed. He tried to sit up and failed.

He began to cry, and choked it off as rapidly as it came. He gathered himself, sucked in fetid air. He *was* going to move. No stinking animal was going to stop him. He felt a strength pouring through him that was almost superhuman.

Now!

He wrenched and twisted to his right, felt the suit roll over. He was clear! He lurched to his feet, his eyes blazed. He stumbled out of the tent, pulling shadow beasts with him.

He could see! The fire in the clearing still burned feebly, and the moon was pouring silver down through the night. The wolf-things were all around him, circling him, moving in again. The muscles rippled on their lean flanks, their jaws were bleeding where they had tried to tear a hole in his suit.

Monte laughed wildly. "Come on, you devils! Come on and fight!"

"Monte! What are you doing?"

"Shut up!"

"Monte, remember——"

"Shut up, I tell you!" He was screaming, he had gone mad.

The wolf-things jumped him, trying for his metallic throat, trying to pull him down. There was no longer any thought in his mind of standing and taking it. He was clumsy in his suit, but he had a strength he hadn't known he possessed. He moved his arms as though they were pistons.

He caught one of the beasts in his gloved left hand, gripping it by the leg. He lifted it off the ground and smashed his right hand into its snarling face. The thing dropped like a stone when he let it go.

He picked up another one, staggering under its weight. He threw it at a tree, hard. He crouched down in his bulky armor, moved forward like a wrestler. His breath whistled in his teeth. He grabbed one that was trying to slink away, swung it in a great circle, and hurled it into the coals of the fire. It hit with a shower of sparks, rolled, and bolted for the safety of the trees.

His own laughter was maniacal in his ears. He seized a log and whirled it around his helmeted head like a scythe. He felt it crunch into something, and it felt good.

"Monte!"

Something had him from behind; he tried to shake it off but couldn't. He pulled free and turned, the log ready in his hands.

Charlie stood there, an impossible robot in the moonlight, waving his arms.

"They've gone!" The voice rang in his ears. "They've gone! Put the log down, you fool! What are you trying to do?"

He hesitated, and that was enough. Something like sanity came back to him. His arms were suddenly as heavy as lead and he dropped the log to the ground. He looked around. The clearing was empty. He saw one of the Merdosini dragging itself into the trees.

"You idiot! They couldn't hurt us. You know what we decided——"

That voice. He had to get away from that voice.

Trembling, he reached up and unlocked his helmet. He jerked it from his head, swallowed the fresh clean air.

Something inside him snapped. He leaned against a

rock and was violently, desperately sick. He couldn't move, didn't want to move.

Charlie stumbled over to him, a gloved hand caught at his shoulder. He tried to brush the hand aside but he didn't have the strength. Charlie picked up his helmet and clamped it down over his head again. All sounds stopped except for the noise of harsh, labored breathing. His? Charlie's?

The tinny voice again. "You take that hat off again and I'll brain you with a rock. What got into you?"

"Don't know, don't know. . . ."

He could hardly stand. Charlie steered him toward the tent.

There was a light. It came from Charlie's suit. He saw that his cot was smashed beyond repair. The tent was a shambles.

The anger poured through him again. He was glad that he had fought back, plan or no plan. He hoped that he had killed a few of them. Somewhere, in some dim corner of his brain, he knew that his thoughts were crazy thoughts—but it didn't matter.

The beasts had attacked them, hadn't they?

"Lie down, Monte. They won't be back tonight." Charlie's voice sounded tired and hopeless, as though he had been let down from an unexpected quarter.

What's the matter with him?

Or is it me? What's the matter with me?

He was on the floor of the tent, on his back. He had no idea how he had gotten there, but it felt wonderful.

He was exhausted. Everything was far away, fuzzy.

"Charlie? Sorry, Charlie. Feel so strange. . . ."

The voice came in from miles away. "Go to sleep. We'll talk about it in the morning."

"Yeah, go to sleep. . . ."

He closed his eyes.

In seconds, he was asleep.

And that, really, was when it started.

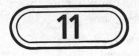

11

D REAMS?
   Monte wasn't at all sure that they were dreams,
which in itself was strange. Somehow, he had always known
when he was dreaming. If the dream had been pleasant, he
had enjoyed it. If it had been one of those terrible dreams
that come welling up from the black pits of the mind—or
from an improvident sandwich eaten too late at night—he
had simply willed himself to wakefulness.

It's just a dream, he would think. *Wake up! End it!*

And he would stir and open his eyes and feel Louise's
warm body next to his and everything would be fine.

But now his dream was very clear, very real. It was not
at all complicated and it had a weird kind of plausibility to
it. He was back home, and it was years ago. For some reason, he had killed a man—a featureless man, a man without
a face. He had dug a hole out in the woods and buried the
man. He had covered up the grave and forgotten about it.
Long years had passed and nobody suspected that he was a
murderer. He hardly knew it himself; he had buried his se-

122

cret deep in his mind and kept it there. And then one day a hunter was building a fire. He cleared away the brush and found a decayed hand sticking out of the earth. He uncovered the rest of the body. The skin-shredded skull spoke the name of Monte Stewart.

They were coming for him, coming to get him. It was all over. The secret was out. He should have confessed years ago. . . .

It's just a dream! Wake up! End it!

He fought his way out of the dream, peeling away the layers of fog and cotton. Sure, it was just a dream! A typical silly guilt dream, even. Calling Dr. Freud!

He stirred, opened his eyes.

He felt Louise's warm body next to his.

Good. It was over.

No! It could not be.

Why, Louise was dead. She couldn't be here. She was cold, cold. . . .

And he had a spacesuit on, didn't he? How could he feel her warm body?

Dreams?

He moaned, not knowing whether he was asleep or awake. He tried to remember. He was in a tent with Charlie. Charlie Jenike. And they had been attacked by great wolf-things with yellow eyes. Why? What had they done?

Wait!

They were coming back again, out of the blackness that crouches just before the dawn. He could hear them padding into the tent. He could smell the animal stink of them. They were on top of him, their gaping jaws tearing at his chest. . . .

He tried to move and could not. He was pinned down. His mouth opened, desperately seeking for the air that was no longer there. Cunningly, he tried to roll over. He didn't move an inch.

They can't get at me. I'm safe in my suit. Remember? He relaxed. Safe!

But what was that, coming silently through the entrance to the tent? What was that long-armed naked shadow? It was bending over him, smiling. . . .

It was unlocking his helmet, pulling it off!

Monte screamed.

A wave of blackness washed over him.

A metallic voice spoke in his ear, coming from far away: "Monte! Lie still! There's nothing after you! Wake up, wake up. . . ."

He opened his wide, staring eyes. There was a robot bending over him. He saw the robot's face.

Charlie.

The gray light of morning was washing into the tent. He was alive.

After three cups of coffee, he was still shivering.

He stood with his back to the fire, knowing that it was foolish even as he did it. He could not feel the fire through his suit, and the early morning air was not really cold. It was damp and the ground was wet, but Sirius was greater than any man-made fire. It rose behind thick gray clouds and its heat was heavy and oppressive.

His eyes were tired and red-rimmed and his beard was a tangled mess. (Beards, he realized, were not ideal equipment inside spacesuit helmets.) He could not have slept more than two or three hours and he was bone-weary.

Still, his brain was working again. His sanity had returned, and he was grateful. Monte Stewart had never been a man to doubt himself before, but now he was unsure. He did not understand his own actions.

And those dreams, if dreams they had been. They were sick dreams. Tired as he was, they alarmed him.

"I don't get it," he said.

Charlie looked like he had not slept at all. He spooned breakfast mush out of a can and kept his distance. "You must have gone off your rocker."

Monte managed a wry smile. "I guess that man is not a very rational animal. We assumed that because we were determined to be fair and peaceful the natives would be the same way. They weren't. And we assumed that I would always act logically. I didn't. Maybe we're two of a kind."

"But why? We made our big speech, we had our plan. We knew that the Merdosini would attack us, and we knew that they couldn't hurt us. All we had to do was to wait until they went away. We would have proved our point—we meant no harm even if we were attacked. And then you blow your stack and fight back. If that's the best we can do we might as well quit."

Monte poured the dregs of his coffee into the fire. "I'm sorry."

"Swell, wonderful. You're sorry. What do we do now? Send them a making-up present?"

"I don't know. What do you think?"

"You're the big genius. This was all your idea. You tell me."

Monte rubbed his tired eyes. He looked at the mocking
trees that surrounded the clearing. The plain truth was that
he had no ideas at all. He had nothing but a hard knot of
determination. He was too worn out to think.

"You won't win any good-conduct medals this morning
yourself," he said irritably. "What's eating you?"

Charlie threw up his hands in despair. "He throws away
the only chance we've got and then he asks me what's eating
me. My God!"

Monte turned and faced him. "I said I was sorry. I'm
not Superman. I make mistakes. I don't know what got into
me. But I do know that if we start knocking each other we're
through. Cut it out."

Charlie sat down heavily on a log. He cupped his chin
in his gloved hands. He seemed infinitely weary. "It's everything, Monte. These damned suits. The miserable air. The
whole stinking planet. I didn't sleep at all last night. Right
now, none of it makes any sense. I don't even know what
I'm doing here. I might as well be on the ship. I just don't
care any longer."

Monte nodded slowly. "It would be easy to quit. It gets
easier all the time. There just doesn't seem to be any logical
reason for going on. I know all that."

"Then why not quit and be done with it?"

"I don't even know the answer to that one. But it's a
hard thing to be defeated, Charlie. It's easy to quit, but you
have to live with it a long, long time."

"Thank you, Friendly Old Philosopher. You've made it
all as clear as mud."

"Maybe you'd better hit the sack for a while. I'll hold
the fort. We won't get anywhere this way."

Charlie pulled himself to his feet. "You twisted my

arm. I can't say that I'm anxious to stick my head in that blasted helmet again, though."

"Do it anyhow."

"Of course." Charlie looked at him strangely, but said nothing more. He picked up his helmet and disappeared into the tent.

Monte stood silently in the gray morning light. There was a smell of rain in the air. He studied the trees but saw nothing suspicious.

Dimly, in the depths of his mind, a thought nagged at him. He tried to pull it out into the open, but it was too much trouble.

He just stood there and looked at nothing, nothing at all.

Along about noon, when the cloud-smothered surface of Sirius Nine was a steaming jungle that threatened to melt Monte in his suit, the gray heavens opened up and a torrent of warm rain turned the clearing into a puddled swamp.

There was no thunder and little wind. The rain hissed down in shimmering sheets, effectively isolating Monte where he stood and masking the forest that surrounded him. It was a peaceful rain and he was slow in reacting to it. He was puzzled at his own feelings. The rain was pleasant against his face and even the slight trickle of water inside his suit was not unwelcome.

I want it to be a magic rain, he thought. *I want it to wash everything away. I want it to cleanse this world. I want it to make me clean again. I want it to make me forget, forget. . . .*

Forget what? He shook his head. *I don't understand*

*myself. Is there something the matter with me, something
the matter with the way I am thinking?*

Sick? I must be sick. But what is it? What is it?

He stood for a long time in the strange shelter of the
rain and then walked over to the tent. He pushed his way
inside. He did not want to leave the rain, but he thought
vaguely that if he were sick he should take some medicine
and the medicine was in the tent. . . .

He waited for a moment, letting his eyes accustom
themselves to the darkness. His suit dripped in little puddles
on the floor. He heard Charlie's labored breathing and realized that Charlie had gone to sleep without his helmet.
That could be dangerous if the Merdosini came back. He
started toward Charlie's cot.

Charlie sat up suddenly, his eyes wild.

"You!" Charlie pointed a trembling finger. "Keep away
from me!"

Monte heard his own voice speaking. It was definitely
his own voice, but it was alienated from him. It was very
much like hearing a playback of his voice from a recording
machine. It said: "Your helmet. You can't sleep without
your helmet."

Charlie lurched to his feet, monstrous in his swollen
suit. His breathing was harsh in the confinement of the tent.
"Get out, get away! I know you now. You can't fool me any
longer."

"You can't sleep without your helmet." (Why did he
keep saying that?)

"Don't touch my helmet, let it alone!"

"You can't sleep——"

"Shut up!" Charlie tried to back away, but there was no
place to go. "It's all your fault—everything is your fault! If it

hadn't been for you, I wouldn't be here. If it hadn't been for you, we wouldn't have made so many stupid mistakes. If it hadn't been for you, Helen would still be alive!"

The words slashed through the fog in Monte's brain like a knife. "Charlie, I lost my wife too—"

"Clever! Oh, you're clever, no doubt about that. You wanted to get rid of her! You dirty murderer. . . ."

"Charlie——"

"Get away! Get back, I warn you. . . ."

Monte tried to run, but he was rooted to the spot. This was insane. If only he could think, if only he could free his mind from whatever it was that held him in thrall.

"I can't stand it!" Charlie crouched down: he was squat and ugly like some prehistoric beast with a scaly reptilian skin. "I won't just stand here and take it!"

"Wait, Charlie." (Charlie? No, surely this was not the Charlie Jenike he had known. What was happening?)

The thing that had been Charlie Jenike attacked.

The sheer hurtling fury of his rush knocked Monte from his feet. He fell heavily to the floor of the tent, he felt immensely strong hands closing about his throat, he heard Charlie snarling like a wild animal to his face.

"Kill you, kill you, kill you!"

Monte doubled his gloved fist and swung a short chopping blow at Charlie's exposed head. There was a crunching thud as he connected. The clutching hands relaxed their pressure against his throat. With a wild surge of power, he heaved the robot-body away from him .

Monte leaped to his feet, ignoring the weight of the suit he wore. His lips curled back in a smile. He walked over and kicked Charlie in the head with his boot.

Charlie began to scream. The sound was very unpleasant. Monte decided to cut it off. He knelt down beside Charlie, reached out, and got him around the neck. He started to squeeze.

The screaming stopped.

"Call me a murderer, will you? You miserable excuse for a human being. . . ."

He tightened his grip. Charlie's eyes were bulging.

Then Monte heard his other voice, the one that whispered inside his brain—a voice miraculously insulated, protected, preserved.

Call me a murderer. . . .

Miserable excuse for a human being. . . .

A wave of revulsion washed over him. He jerked his hands away from Charlie's throat as though they had touched the fires of hell.

My God, what have I done?

"Charlie! Charlie!"

Charlie gasped for breath. He looked up with the most bewildered, tortured eyes that Monte had ever seen. The eyes were wild and stricken, but there was the light of sanity in them.

"Help me," Charlie whispered hoarsely. "Help me!"

Monte pulled him into a sitting position, then threw his arm across his shoulder and hauled him to his feet.

"Charlie! I don't know what's going on, I can't think. But we have to get out of here! Now, this minute!"

"Yes, help me. . . ."

Together, they staggered out of the tent into the gray hiss of the rain. They didn't know where they were going, or why. They had lost everything, even their hope.

They knew only that they had to get away.

Fast. Before it was too late. Before it was all over.

They stumbled through the rain, two shapeless monsters spawned in a nightmare of desolation. They walked and crawled into the dark, dripping forest and disappeared.

Where the men from Earth had been, there was only an empty clearing in the rain.

An empty clearing and a dead fire and two sagging tents and two forgotten spacesuit helmets. . . .

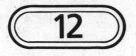

R UN! Monte felt the blood pounding in his head. The very air that he breathed seared his lungs; his chest heaved in shuddering gasps inside the prison of his suit. He slipped and fell sprawling in the mud. He lurched back to his feet and kept on going.

Run!

He had no destination: he was running away from something, not toward something. He was running away from the rain-soaked clearing, running away from the dark long-armed shadows of the Merdosi, running away from the wolf-things that prowled in the night.

And he was running away from himself.

Run!

The jungle of trees around him became an impenetrable wall; he had to fight for light, for air. Creepers and vines and thickets snatched at his boots. He could see nothing clearly. Even the leaden gray sky was invisible. There was nothing in all the world but the fury of flight, nothing but the mindless command to keep on going, always, forever.

Dimly, he was aware of the crashing of a heavy body behind him, a sound of boots sucking at the mud, a sound of shallow choking gasps for air.

Come on, Charlie! Don't give up! Run!

He crashed out of the trees into the half-light of the fading day. Through a screen of silver rain he saw a brown, swollen river. It gushed between eroding banks and foamed against glistening upthrust boulders. The water was as black as dirty oil, except where the surface was cut by rocks and the white spray leaped into the air. The booming of the river filled the world; there was nothing else.

He knew that he had to cross the river. It was desperately important to him that he get to the other side. But how? Swimming in the spacesuit was out of the question; he would sink like a stone. Even if he threw away the suit he could never swim in that rushing water.

Reluctantly, he stopped. He fell to his knees, fighting for breath. Charlie staggered out of the forest behind him and fell full-length on the ground, sobbing.

There *had* to be a way.

Somehow, he got to his feet. He walked upstream, staring at the thrust of the water. Behind the gray curtain of the rain, the boulders in the river bed glistened like naked primordial islands. A wall of sound beat at his ears. But every atom of his being was bent toward a single goal:

Run!

Get across the river!

He kept on going, his eyes narrowed against the rain. He hauled the senseless spacesuit with him as thoughtlessly as a turtle carries the shell upon his back.

There. He blinked his eyes. The river widened, fanning out between crumbling banks of yellow mud. Massive rocks loomed up out of the foaming water like a chain of battered islands that stretched from bank to bank. The river ran fast and rough in silver-laced rapids, but it was not deep. He could walk across on the boulders if he didn't slip. If he did miss his footing. . . .

Well, that would be that.

He didn't look back; he simply assumed that Charlie was there. His boots squished through the sticky mud and he scrambled out upon the first rock. It was slippery with slime; he had to keep moving or fall. The spray drenched his face, making it hard for him to breathe. But the noise was the worst. The nameless river roared at him with an ancient chant of malevolent fury.

Like some misshapen, unrecorded beast from a forgotten era, he scrambled along from rock to rock. He could hardly see where he was going and he was driven on by a mad, unreasoning will that had possessed his body. He clawed at the slick rocks with his thick-gloved fingers, kicked at them with his boots, hugged them with his arms. He cursed them, reviled them, screamed at them.

He fell the last few feet, fell into dirty rushing water that rolled him over like a log. He crawled to the shore and flopped out of the water like the first amphibian groping for the land.

The river was behind him. He had crossed the river. He was too weak to stand. He lay in the mud, smiling insanely.

He heard someone screaming hysterically. He twisted around and saw Charlie's bloated body doing a crazy tight-rope dance across the chain of boulders. He wanted to help him but he could hardly move. He slithered around in the mud until he was facing the river again and stretched out his hands. When Charlie fell from the last rock he caught him and pulled him out of the water.

Charlie lay face-down in the yellow mud, his body heaving convulsively. Gradually, his movements subsided. He turned his mud-streaked face toward Monte and tried to smile.

"We made it," he whispered. "I don't believe it."

Monte took a deep breath; his demon was driving him on. "Can't stay here."

"Good a place as any. We're through."

"Find a dry place. Hole up."

"What for?"

Monte was impatient with talk. Didn't the man *know* that they had to keep on going? Couldn't he *see* that they had to get away from the river? Didn't he understand that they had to find. . . .

What?

Monte pulled himself slowly to his feet. A part of him was amazed that he could stand, but another part of him knew that there were dark reservoirs of strength in his body that no machine could ever measure, no man could ever comprehend.

For a moment, he blacked out. Then the blood came back to his head and he swayed with dizziness. Despite the mud and the rain he felt hot.

Probably burning up with fever. But what does that mean? What is fever? Just a word. Words can't help me now. There are no words.

"Come on, Charlie," he said. "Get up."

"Can't."

"You can. Get up. It won't be far."

"We're beaten."

Monte reached down, caught Charlie under the arms, and heaved him to his feet. "You can't stay here."

Charlie shook his head. "I can't go on."

"You can. Just *do* it."

Monte turned and started away from the river. He concentrated on putting one foot in front of the other. He did not look back. He did not think. He just kept walking beneath a weeping sky, drawn as a metal filing is drawn toward a magnet that it cannot see.

The country was open now, exposed to the sweep of the rain. He walked through tall grass, trampling down the wet spears with his boots. He could feel the land rising under him, and far ahead, masked by the gray curtain of the rain, he saw the high horizon. A jagged and dark horizon that held the edge of the coming night.

Mountains.

He did not know how long it took him to reach the foothills; time had lost its meaning. He might have walked forever under the alien sky with the night wind in his face. But he did not stop. He simply endured. He kept on going.

It was quite dark and the rain still fell. He looked up at banks of cliffs and saw it there. A deeper blackness against the single shadow of the night. A doorway of darkness. . . .

A cave.

He smiled. He had not known what it was that he was searching for, but he knew it when he saw it. A cave. That was it. That was the answer.

It *had* to be.

He climbed a twisting trail up the face of the cliff. He could hear Charlie behind him, dislodging rocks with his boots. He reached the mouth of the cave. He did not hesitate. He bent down and edged inside. It was black, black as midnight in a land that had never known the light of the stars, but it was warm and dry.

He was safe. He knew he was safe.

He moved back from the entrance and fell on the floor. He found a flat rock to use for a pillow. He closed his eyes.

He knew somehow that a cycle had ended. He had come full circle.

Charlie collapsed beside him, gasping with exhaustion. Monte's brain tried to tell him that he should not sleep, but it was no use.

It did not matter.

Nothing mattered.

He was safe, safe in the cave that was the beginning of all men, hidden from the world beyond.

He slept.

The strange, twisted dreams did not return. He slept the heavy sleep of complete and utter weariness. Gradually, his breathing became regular. The lines in his face smoothed and softened. His body relaxed.

When he woke up, Monte saw a golden haze at the mouth of the cave. The sun was up and the rain had stopped. Even inside the cavern, the air smelled fresh and fragrant. At first, he did not move. He just lay where he was, rejoicing in the simple pleasure of being alive.

No, it was more than that. He was not only alive. He

was well. The fevered sickness that had chained his mind
was gone, washed away. He felt cleansed and happy. It was
perhaps the oldest and most fundamental of all human joys:
*I have been sick, and now I am well. I have stood on the
brink of the black pit, and I have come back.*

Sanity. It was something that Monte had always taken
for granted. Madness had never been something that could
happen to *him*. Others, yes. But not to him.

Now, he knew better. He was thankful just to be himself.

But what had happened to him—and to Charlie? Was
it possible that they had been on Sirius Nine for just two
nights? It seemed to him that those few hours had been an
eternity, longer than all the rest of his life. He could not
even remember them clearly. It was all so jumbled, so confused. . . .

And there was something about the whole experience,
something that he could not quite remember. A quality of
desperate urgency, of testing, of menace. It had not been
natural. It was somehow intimately bound up with the in-
comprehensible Merdosi, and with the wolf-things, and
with the dark shadows of the unsuspected. . . .

He got to his feet, moving quietly so as not to disturb
Charlie. He crouched down and walked to the mouth of the
cave. He stepped outside.

The white furance of Sirius struck him like a blow, but
he welcomed it—welcomed the heat and the light and the
purity of it. He reveled in the sweep of the blue sky, the
rain-washed green of the grasses, the flame of the red leaves
on the trees. The fresh air kissed his face. Even the distant
river was peaceful, winding its way between yellow banks,
gleaming like glass in the hot rays of the sun.

He looked at himself, fingered the tangle of his matted beard. His suit was caked with mud. There was a great jagged tear in his left leg. His gloves were scratched and stiff. His body felt damp and infested with filth.

Slowly, Monte began to remove the spacesuit. The gloves went first, and he noticed that his hands were white and clammy, as though they had been too long away from the light of the sun. He struggled with the suit, taking it off section by section. It wasn't an easy job. When he had finished, the suit lay crumpled on the rocks like a discarded serpent skin.

He took off the rest of his damp clothing and stretched it out on a flat stone to dry. The heat of the sun felt wonderful, and it was with reluctance that he moved back into a shadow to get out of the glare. He knew that Sirius could blister his naked skin in a few short minutes. Still, it was a real temptation to linger awhile in the bright light.

He wanted a bath. A bath, he decided, was one of the great unappreciated blessings of civilization. A bath and a good meal and a cool drink. . . .

Well, all that would have to wait. It was something just to get rid of the spacesuit. He looked at the thing with active dislike. The whole idea of the spacesuits, which had seemed so logical on the ship, was utterly wrong. It was wrong, and yet it was completely characteristic of the mistakes that he had made. How could you expect to contact a people by insulating yourself from them?

Somehow, he needed a new way of thinking. He needed a fresh approach. He needed to think the whole thing out with an uncluttered mind.

He sat down on a rock, cupping his bearded chin in his hands. He looked out at the panorama of the world below him. It was hard to believe that there was ugliness in all that beauty, hard to believe that evil could exist in such a place.

There had to be an answer somewhere. There had to be a key that would unlock Sirius Nine. There had to be some path that he could follow, a path that would lead not only to an understanding of the Merdosi but also to an understanding of himself and what he represented. . . .

That was when he heard the terrible sound.

He leaped to his feet, his reverie forgotten.

Inside the cave, Charlie was screaming.

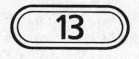

13

F OR A MOMENT a pang of despair shot through him and he abandoned himself to it. He had assumed that Charlie too would be free of the sickness, although there was no real reason for thinking so. It seemed to him that he was miserably alone, miserably helpless. He was faced with a task that was beyond his powers. He was making no progress at all.

The awful screaming continued. There were no words in it; it wasn't human. It was a naked animal cry of agony.

Monte pulled himself together. He didn't know how he did it, just as he didn't know what it was that had carried him through the past night of horror. He only knew that he was an actor in some vast and terrible drama and that he must play his part until he dropped.

He ducked down and went into the cave. There was plenty of light and he could see clearly. Charlie was on his back, his swollen arms sticking straight up into the air, his gloved fists tightly clenched. His dirty face was contorted and sweating, his mouth loose and trembling.

The screams filled the cave.

Monte knelt down, ready for anything. He felt as though he were caught up in some endlessly repeating cycle with no way out, no way to break the chain.

He slapped Charlie's face, hard.

"Wake up! You're dreaming. It's okay. You're safe. Everything's okay. Wake up!"

The screaming stopped. Charlie snorted and opened his eyes. The eyes were wild with terror, filled with a nameless fear.

"It's okay, Charlie. You've been dreaming. It's just me, Monte. Easy does it, boy. Relax. Take it easy."

Charlie looked at him. Gradually, the light of recognition dawned in his eyes. His arms dropped to his chest. He shook his head, licked his lips.

"It's all over, Charlie. Don't let it get you. Look—see the sun shining out there? We're okay."

Charlie stared at Monte's nakedness. Suddenly, he smiled. "What is this, a nudist colony? Now I know I'm nuts!"

Monte laughed with relief. Charlie seemed to be himself again. "I just couldn't stand that damned suit any longer. Come on outside and get yours off. You'll feel better."

Charlie didn't move.

"Come on, get up. We'll get us some food. . . ."

Charlie shuddered and seemed to withdraw into his suit as a turtle will pull its head back into its shell. Monte reached out and touched his shoulder, trying to pull him back from wherever he was going.

"There's nothing to be afraid of now. Don't let it get you again. Fight it!"

"No."

"Man, you can't give up! Look out there—the sun is shining——"

"Damn the sun. What difference does it make? Not *our* sun."

"What's wrong with you? What's the matter? Let me help. . . ."

Charlie closed his eyes. His breathing was very shallow. "I tried to kill you, Monte. Have you forgotten that?"

Monte waved his hand irritably. "We were sick. They did something to us. We weren't responsible. That wasn't *us* fighting. Don't you know that?"

"Words." Charlie opened his haunted eyes. "My God, the things I saw in my mind! The dreams I had! Am I like that?"

"Of course not."

"Those things came out of my mind. Things about you and Louise. Even about Helen. Slime! Sick? Lord, the sickness is inside us. I don't know myself. All the things you keep bottled up inside of you and then somebody takes the lid off. We tried to kill each other! And you say that everything is fine. Mad! We're both mad!"

"Maybe so. But this won't get us anywhere. We've got to fight!"

"Fight what? Shadows? Dreams? A planet? Ourselves? Go away. Let me alone. I don't want to do anything else, ever."

"Come on outside. The fresh air will do you good."

Charlie laughed—a bitter, hollow, broken laugh. "Fresh air! That's funny."

"Dammit, I'm trying to help you! Charlie, we're all alone here. We can't quit. There's too much at stake."

"Garbage, garbage. Idiocy. We should have quit before we started. Helen's dead. Louise is dead. Ralph is dead. We'll be dead soon. And for what? For what? Hang the Merdosi! They're not like us, never have been, never will be. They're monsters. We're monsters!"

"You're contradicting yourself. Come on, now. . . ."

A look of cunning came into Charlie's sunken eyes. "No. They're out there. All around us. I can feel them. They're after me, inside my head."

Monte was baffled in the presence of the sickness that he saw in the other man. It was like talking to a lunatic. "I've been out there. I've looked. We're all alone."

"I can feel them, I tell you! Do you really think you can get away from them by splashing across a river? This is their world, not ours. We're finished!"

Monte searched desperately for some magic words that would get through to him. There were no words.

Charlie sighed, closed his eyes again. He went down into the depths of some profound depression. He began to mumble, to whisper, to cry. "No good. I'm no good. The things I saw—in my own mind—I'm sick, so sick. . . ."

"Do you want me to contact the ship?" Monte asked quietly. "You can't go on like this—it's asking too much of any man. Maybe it would be best——"

"No, no. Can't go back, nothing there. Can't leave you here. Just let me alone, can't you? Let me rest—think. . . ."

Monte got to his feet. "You need something to eat. I'll get some."

"Don't go out there! Don't leave me! Stay here!"

"Starving never appealed to me much," Monte said firmly. "We have to get food. You wait here, do you understand? I'll be back."

Charlie began to cry again.

Monte walked out into the sunlight and put on his warm, dry clothes. He unhooked the spare canteen from the spacesuit and fastened it to his belt. He tried not to listen to the wretched sobbing from the cave.

He started down the trail toward the green world below.

The whispering grasslands surrounded him and the smell of the rain-washed air was sweet. The land sloped gently toward the river and the sky above his head was warm and blue and comforting. In spite of himself, in spite of everything, Monte felt a sudden surge of confidence.

He could take it. He knew that now, and it was a valuable thing to know. A man could go all through his life and never meet the final test that would tell him what he was. When all the horrors are behind you there is nothing more to fear.

How in the devil was he going to get his hands on some food? The water was easy; he could simply go on to the river and fill his canteen. But he had no weapons. He was not eager to go back to the clearing and pick up some cans, although it might come to that in the end. He might build a trap of some sort, but that was a slow and uncertain technique at best.

He remembered that Ralph had run some tests on a batch of red berries that he had picked. If he could find some of those it might help. But a man couldn't live on berries. Roots? Fish?

Well, first things first. He kept on toward the river, enjoying the walk, strangely at ease. The world of Walonka no longer seemed alien to him; it was even beautiful, once you

got used to it. Perhaps all worlds were beautiful to apprecia-
tive eyes. Planets were not alien, at least not the ones a man
could walk on without an artificial air supply. People were
the problem. It was far easier to adjust to a new world than
to a new human being.

He stepped out of the grass and saw the river gliding
before him, quiet and peaceful in the bright sunlight. It was
a far cry from the wild torrent of the night before; even the
upthrust rocks looked dry and inviting. He stretched out on
the cool bank and put his mouth in the water. He drank. It
tasted clean and fresh. He filled his canteen and wished fervently that he had not left his pipe and tobacco back in the
tent. He could do with a smoke. In fact, despite his empty
belly, he would have been completely content with his pipe.
He had always loved the land, any land that had not been
spoiled by the stinks of civilization, and a man could ask for
very little more than a clean river and a blue sky and a warm
sun.

He felt completely at peace with himself.

Perhaps the river was the answer. There had to be fish
in it, hanging in those dark pools by the rocks. As an old
fisherman, he could almost *smell* fish. He could rig up a line
of some sort, bait it with insects or even berries, catch himself a mess of fish. . . .

And he suddenly remembered the birds. It should not
be too difficult to locate some nests, swipe a few eggs. He
smiled. If only that was all there was to life! Enough to eat,
enough to drink, a fire to keep you warm, a shelter to keep
you dry, a little love. . . .

How did the lives of men get so complicated? Why did
men insist on cluttering up their lives with all the little irri-

tations that made a man old before his time? Why couldn't a guy just sit in the sun and fish and smoke his pipe?

He didn't know. But he was not simple enough to believe in his own lotus dream. He recognized it for what it was: a reaction to all the hell he had been through, a fantasy of all the Good Old Days that never had been. There was some truth in it, sure. Maybe even a little wisdom. But a man was what he was. He had a brain and he couldn't switch it on and off at will.

Louise was dead. Charlie was sobbing in a cave in some nameless cliff. He, Monte, had failed in his job. The Earth and Sirius Nine had touched across the dark seas of space, and their destinies were bound together forever—no enchanted Excalibur could cut the chains that tied them. There was a vast and intricate play of forces at work here and now, by this peaceful river, and they all centered on him. He had to do what he could, or forget about calling himself a man.

He got to his feet, then froze.

There was an animal drinking from the river not twenty yards downstream from him. It was a lovely creature, not unlike a deer, but it was small and its legs were short. It was not built for speed like a deer. There were no horns on its head. Its coat was a soft brown with flecks of white. It was very dainty, and it was—helpless.

The animal looked up at Monte, took him in with gentle liquid eyes, and did not move. It didn't seem frightened. It nibbled at the green shoots of a bush that grew along the river bank and twitched its short tail lazily.

Probably, Monte thought, the animal had confused him with one of the natives. The wind was blowing in

Monte's face, and without the clue of scent the animal did not realize that he was anything strange. And the natives always hunted with the Merdosini. . . .

If he could catch him, break his neck—or even stun him with a rock. . . .

Monte took a step toward the animal. The animal eyed him curiously and continued to munch on the grass. Monte moved closer, careful to make no sudden motions. The creature sniffed the air. Its mule ears cocked forward along its head.

Monte held his breath. Fifteen yards to go. Ten.

The animal backed away. It gave a kind of whistling snort, turned, and trotted off through the high grass. It wasn't really running. Just keeping its distance.

Monte suddenly realized that he was very hungry. There was a lot of meat on that critter. He picked up a stone about the size of a baseball. If he could just get a little closer. . . .

Monte broke into an easy run, bringing his feet down as softly as he could. The animal didn't look back, but matched his pace. Monte braced himself, deciding that a quick sprint was his only chance. He gripped the stone firmly. Now. . . .

Just as he started to race forward, he saw it.

He dropped like a shot, hiding himself in the tall grass.

He was not the only one hunting that animal. One of the wolf-things, belly low to the ground, swift and silent as death itself, was cutting across the trail.

Monte parted the grass and watched. How could he have been so careless? He was completely helpless without the protection of his suit—as helpless as that runt deer. But the wolf-thing didn't seem to be interested in him; he went after his prey with a single-minded concentration that was frightening to observe.

The little animal never knew what hit him. The Merdosini struck like a blur, like a soundless shadow. The great white fangs ripped at the jugular and there was a spurt of crimson blood that reddened the muzzle of the killer. It was all over in seconds.

That was when the man stepped out of the grass and whistled. Monte's eyes widened in surprise. He knew that man. He was an old man, tall and long-armed and naked with vertical stripes of vermillion on his chest. His skin was copper in the sunlight and the fine hair on his head was a fuzz of gold. And his eyes, those dark and tortured eyes— Monte couldn't forget them.

It was the same old man that they had first tried to contact after the landing on Sirius Nine. The old man who had fled from his hollow tree when they had tried to talk to him—how long ago? What was he doing here, on this side of the river?

The man called off the wolf-thing. The beast whined and rubbed up against the old man's legs in an oddly doglike gesture. The man patted his head absently, then reached down, gathered up the dead animal, and hoisted it to his shoulders. From where he lay in the grass, Monte could distinctly see the red blood trickling down over the copper skin.

Side by side, the man and the wolf-thing set off through the high grass.

They were headed straight for the cliff where the cave was. Coincidence? Monte hardly thought so.

He thought fast. It wouldn't do to make any foolish mistakes this time. The old man wasn't much of a threat to them as long as he was alone. And the wolf-thing was probably safe enough as long as the old man controlled him. If Monte let himself be seen, he might scare the old man away. He didn't want that. It was just possible. . . .

He waited until they had a good lead on him. He waited until he was sure that the long grass would conceal his movements. Then he got to his feet and silently followed their trail.

He walked through the green world under the white sun.

Hope was reborn in him.

He followed the trail of the old man and the killer. Each step he took brought him closer to the foothills of the mountains where Charlie waited in the cave.

And each step he took filled him with wonder.

14

THE OLD MAN walked steadily beneath his burden, the long muscles of his body seeming to flow as he moved. He did not stop to rest. The wolf-thing padded along at his side, occasionally even frisking in front of its master.

A man and his dog, Monte thought. A man and his dog packing out a deer. How easy it was to transpose this scene into an earthly parallel! Psychologically, it was a dangerous line of reasoning—and yet it had a certain validity to it. Offhand, to someone who had never been there, it might seem that the life-forms of Sirius Nine should be totally different in appearance from those of Earth. But wasn't that notion violently contradicted by all the facts of evolution? It was one of those insidiously logical ideas that suffered from one minor flaw: it wasn't true. Even a nodding acquaintance with terrestrial evolution should have been enough to puncture that particular bubble. One of the most arresting facts of evolution was the principle of parallelism or convergence. Life-forms that had been separate for millions of years often showed striking similarities. He thought of the classic exam-

151

ple of the marsupials and the placentals. There were marsupial bears, cats, dogs, squirrels—everything. There were creatures that looked like elephants but weren't. And even the history of man illustrated the same idea. Man had almost certainly developed not once, but several times. There were types like *Pithecanthropus* in Java and China and Africa. There were classic Neanderthals living at the same time as *Homo sapiens,* and even interbreeding with them in Palestine and Czechoslovakia. There were many different groups of Miocene primates, such as the *Dryopithecines,* who were evolving in man-like directions. Perhaps there were only a limited number of solutions to the problems of survival. Perhaps a given type of life, such as a mammal, would of necessity develop along parallel lines, no matter where the evolution took place. Perhaps the twin mechanisms of mutation and natural selection would always ensure the survival of basically efficient types: fish and birds, turtles and rabbits, butterflies and men. Perhaps on all the Earth-like planets in the universe, given the proper conditions of air and sunlight and water, man would find only variations on a single master plan. . . .

Alien? Sure, the life on a planet could be alien—Monte had found that out in the nightmare with the Merdosi. But wasn't it alien in its nuances, in its shadings, in its almost-but-not-quite quality? Wasn't it alien because it was subtly different? And wasn't that more truly alien, say, than something that looked like an octopus but had thought patterns just like a modern American?

Take that old man there, walking along under a white sun with a carcass on his back. His bodily proportions were different from Monte's, but so what? The puzzle lay elsewhere. Why was he doing what he was doing? What was he thinking about? What had motivated him to kill that animal and carry it toward the cave? What had it cost him in pain and worry and courage?

What *was* he doing?

Wait and see, boy. Wait and see.

Without hesitation, the old man started up the trail that led to the cave. There could be no doubt that he was familiar with the place; their sanctuary had not been as safe as they had imagined. Monte hung back, not wishing to show himself. He wanted to see what would happen. He listened carefully, but he could not hear Charlie. Asleep? Watching?

Moving quickly from rock to rock, Monte moved up the cliff. He angled off to the left so that he would come out just above and to one side of the cave.

Holding his breath, he wriggled forward and looked down. The old man was standing on the ledge just in front of the cave. The wolf-thing was whining and sniffling at the discarded spacesuit. The man put the dead animal down at the mouth of the cave. For the first time, he hesitated. He backed off a few steps. He folded his long arms across his vermillion-striped chest. He took a deep breath.

The old man spoke. There was a tremor in his voice. He was afraid, but he was determined to do what he had come here to do. He spoke slowly and distinctly, choosing his words with care. Monte had no trouble in understanding him.

"Strangers!" (Literally: "People-Who-Are-Not-Merdosi.") "I speak to you as once you spoke to me. I bring you a gift of food as once you brought me a gift of food. I speak

my name: Volmay. There has been much trouble since you
first spoke to me. Much of it has been due to my own cow-
ardice. It is time for a beginning-again. I tell you my name:
Volmay. Will you speak with me?"

He was answered by silence. Charlie said nothing at all.

Monte cursed to himself. This was the chance they had
been waiting for. Couldn't Charlie see that? He wanted to
show himself, call down to Volmay. But if he startled him
now. . . .

"Strangers! Are you there? I speak my name again: Volmay. I have brought food to you. I am alone. Do you no
longer wish to speak?"

Words! First it was the men of Earth calling out to the
Merdosi. Then it was Volmay calling out to the men of
Earth. And there were never any replies. The gap was never
bridged.

Come on, Charlie! Give him a chance!

The old man stood alone on the ledge of rock, surrounded by the ancient mountains and the sweep of the sky.
The warm wind whispered in the silence.

"Strangers! It is not easy for a man to think against his
people. I am only a man. My courage is weak. Soon I will
go. Will you not speak with me?"

Silence.

Then—sound.

Movement.

Charlie hurtled out of the mouth of the cave as though
shot from a cannon. He was screaming like a madman. His
swollen suit was encrusted with filth, his face was contorted
into a grimace of fury. He had a sharp rock in his hand.

Before Monte could move, Charlie had thrown himself

on the old man. He knocked him down, leaped on top of him. He struck with the rock. The old man jerked his head away and the rock grazed his shoulder, cutting a red gash.

The wolf-thing snarled and circled, its belly low. The old man cried out to him, waved him away. Charlie lifted the rock to strike again.

There was no time to think. Monte jumped down from where he was hidden, fell, and scrambled forward. He grabbed Charlie's arm, twisted it.

"You damn fool! Let him alone!"

"Come to kill us! Get him, get him, don't let him get away!"

Charlie twisted free. He kicked the old man in the head with his boot, stunning him. The wolf-thing growled, fangs bared.

Monte leaped to his feet, threw a punch with his right hand. He connected with the chest plate of Charlie's suit, almost breaking his fist, Charlie swayed off-balance.

"Stop it! He came to help us!"

Charlie shook his head, his eyes wild. He lifted the rock. "Stay away! Keep out of it!" He turned toward the helpless man.

Monte felt as though he were back in the nightmare again, fighting his own kind, fighting himself. But he knew what he had to do.

"Let him alone, Charlie," he said quietly. "Let him alone or I'll kill you."

Charlie hesitated. He took a step toward Monte, then stopped. A look of utter bewilderment passed over his sweating face. The rock fell out of his hand. "No," he said. "I can't—I don't—I don't know. . . ."

Then a strangled sob broke loose from him. He turned and ran down the trail, not even looking where he was going. It was a miracle that he didn't fall.

"Charlie! Come back!"

The awkward figure thrashed its way down the cliff, never pausing for a second. It ran full tilt into the grasslands and vanished.

Monte was caught in the middle. He didn't know what to do. He ignored the whining wolf-thing and knelt by Volmay's side. The old man's eyes were open. His naked body was trembling with shock.

"Are you well?" Monte asked, fumbling with the native language. "I am so—regretful. My friend—he is sick. . . ."

"I know. I will live."

"I must go after him, bring him back. Will you wait?"

The old man spoke slowly. "It always comes to this, to sadness. I tried very hard."

"Yes, yes, I understand you. It is not too late——"

"Who knows? My dreams have been uneasy. We have both done wrong. We cannot trust one another. My dreams told me that we might have a beginning-again, but the dreams are so strange since you have come. . . ."

"Volmay, will you wait? *Will you wait?*"

"It was not easy for me to come here. I do not know. I will try. I will try. . . ."

Monte touched the old man's shoulder. "We are grateful for what you have done. I will be back soon. Wait for me."

"We will do what we must, all of us."

Monte couldn't wait any longer. Charlie was sick; there was no telling what he might do.

He left the old man where he was and ran back down the trail, toward the green world that had swallowed the man who had been his friend, toward the river.

Monte plunged into the tall grasses. It was easy to follow the trail left by Charlie's heavy boots but it was not necessary. He knew where Charlie was going, knew it as certainly as he had ever known anything in his life.

He did not waste his breath in calling. It was too late for words and he needed to conserve what strength he had left. He was weak with hunger. The nervous energy that had sustained him was beginning to falter.

He was covered with sweat when he reached the river. He saw Charlie at once: a squat, bulbous figure on a rock in the middle of the stream. A pathetic, broken man smothering in the shell of his mechanical suit, looking down at the cool, clean water.

Why did he wait for me? Was it too hard to die alone?

"Charlie! Don't do it!" His voice was very small, lost in the immensity of the sky, drowned by the rush of the river.

Charlie Jenike looked back at him and said nothing.

Monte started across the rocks toward him.

Charlie smiled a little, a strangely peaceful smile, and jumped. He hit the water feet first and dropped like a stone. He came up again once, caught in the current. His clumsy body thrashed in the water. He seemed to be trying to swim.

Monte dove into the water, knowing that it was no use. The river was swift and cold. He struck out for the struggling figure but he never had a chance.

Charlie went down again and stayed down.

Monte fished down from the surface, peering through the cool green depths. He stayed down until his lungs were bursting, surfaced, and went down again. He couldn't find him. There were deep pools in the river and the current was swift, swift. . . .

He kept at it until there was no longer any hope and then fought his way to shore. He dragged himself out on the yellow bank and caught his breath. The river looked calm and untroubled under the arch of the sky. There was no sign of Charlie.

He felt empty, completely drained of all emotion. He was exhausted by everything he had been through. He tried to remember Charlie as Charlie had been: a brusque, unkempt man, a man devoted to his subject, a man of integrity, a funny little guy who looked like a penguin. . . .

But that Charlie was far away, far away. He had died—when? Days ago, a lifetime ago. The sick, frightened, bewildered man that had thrown himself into the river had not been Charlie. He had been someone else, a broken man, a man who could not face the dark depths of his own being.

I brought him here. I brought all of them here. Charlie, Louise, Helen, Ralph.

And now I am alone.

And I too have changed. . . .

He looked up into the cloudless blue sky. Somewhere up there a ship still sailed. A mighty ship that had crossed the gulfs between the worlds. A ship that held his people, wondering, waiting. . . . It always came down to human beings. Small, afraid, uncertain, powerless—but it was up to them. It was always up to them.

Monte turned his back on the river and began to retrace

his steps. He was desperately tired. The white sun was dropping down toward the edge of the mountains and the day was hot and still and empty.

He climbed the trail that wound up the cliff. He reached the cave. He thought of it as his home; it was the only home he had.

The old man was gone. The wolf-thing was gone.

The dead animal was still there.

Monte sighed. He made himself go back down and gather wood. He built a small fire by the mouth of the cave and broiled a chunk of meat on a stick. The fat sizzled when it dropped into the fire. The smell of the cooking meat was a good smell. That, at least, had not changed.

He ate until the pain left his belly. He stood on the rocky ledge and watched the great night paint its shadows across the world of Walonka. He took a final swallow of water from his canteen and crawled into his cave.

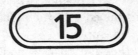

15

THE SUNRISE WAS a glory.

Light flooded the cave and Monte woke up instantly. There was no transition, no fuzziness. He was fresh and alert the moment he opened his eyes, as though just being alive was a great gift and there was no time to waste.

And I was the guy who always needed three cups of coffee to get going!

He stepped out of the cave, drinking in the beauty of the dawn.

The white ball of the sun was drapcd in clouds. It burned through the mist, shining like a rainbow. It reached down with fiery fingers and painted colors on the land: vivid green, flame red, jet black. It bounced its light off the mountains, making them gleam like glass. Its warmth sent a pleasant tingle through his body.

Monte hauled up more wood and built himself a fire. He took a long drink from his canteen and hacked out another chunk of meat from the dead animal. He used a sharp rock to clean the hide away and cooked an ample breakfast.

The meat tasted like venison. It was tough and wild and juicy.

When he had eaten, he found a hard rock to use as a hammerstone and chipped out a reasonably good hand axe. He put a sharp edge on it, leaving the core of the original stone for a grip. He looked at it and grinned. He was making progress. Hell, he was in the Lower Paleolithic already! Another week or two and he could invent pressure flaking. . . .

He went to work on what was left of the meat. He cut it into long narrow strips and put it in the sun to dry. He walked down into the grasslands and found some of the red berries. He pounded the berries into the meat, melted some fat and poured it over the dry meat. He smiled with satisfaction. It probably wasn't the best pemmican in the world, but it would last him for a couple of days.

That was all he needed.

He sat cross-legged in front of his cave, looking down on the land below. The time had come. It was now or never.

He closed his mind to everything except the problem before him. He had all the facts he needed, all the facts he could possibly expect. He had all the pieces of his puzzle. All he had to do was to put them together.

Only—where did you start?

Well, take it from the beginning. Go over it step by step. Think it through.

There must be a key.

There *had* to be a key.

Start with Mark Heidelman who had first told him about Sirius Nine. Was that the beginning? No—go back still further. Go back to the dawn of man on the planet Earth. Go back. . . .

Suddenly, he got to his feet. He looked around him, his eyes staring.

I've been blind. Blind. Here it is, right in front of me!

Yes.

A cave.

A fire.

And a chipped-stone tool.

He picked up the chunk of flaked rock that had become a hand axe. He held it in his hand, held it so tightly that his knuckles whitened.

A chipped-stone tool.

The beginning.

The key.

EXTRACT FROM THE NOTEBOOK OF MONTE STEWART:

This journal looks like something dug up out of a tomb. It's a miracle that it still hangs together. I suppose that no one will ever read what I write here, but somehow that doesn't seem to matter very much. Or does it? Maybe a man always needs to try to communicate—with himself, if necessary.

Communication.

In a way, that's what this whole thing is all about.

I'm excited now. I think I see the answer. I must try to get it down. And then perhaps. . . .

Once you see this thing in perspective, it's not difficult. The trick is to back off; take a long look down the corridors of time. Lord! Isn't it odd how a man can teach an idea for half of his life and then not apply it when the chips are down? I tossed it off every semester in my introductory lecture: "If you want to understand the human animal, you must go back to the beginning. Written records are very recent in the story of man— they only take you back a few thousand years. Man himself has been around for more than to a million years. In order to get an insight into what he is like today, you must look back down that long road and see where he has been. You must go back to the beginning. . . ."

The beginning?

After all, how do we know the story of man on Earth? How did we unravel the past?

We did it by digging up tools. Stone tools.

Paleolithic: Old Stone Age.

Mesolithic: Middle Stone Age.

Neolithic: New Stone Age.

We're so used to it we don't even think about it. It's a part of us. Of course! Who questions the basic dictates of his culture? It always seems so natural, so inevitable.

From the very first, as soon as man became man, he made tools. He chipped artifacts out of stone. This was how he lived. This was how he hunted, how he defended himself, even how he expressed himself. (Who can look at a Solutrean blade and not know that it is a work of art?)

Obvious?

Maybe. But consider this. When man on Earth first started down that trail, there was no turning back. When he chipped his first tool, he determined his destiny. All the rest flowed from that one creative act: spears, harpoons, bows and arrows, the plow, wheels, writing, cities, planes, bombs, spaceships. . . .

It was a way of life, a way of thinking.

It was man's path on Earth.

(It is not for me to say whether that path was good or bad. I don't know whether or not the terms have meaning in this context. But it is a fact, surely, that man saddled himself with a heavy load when he chipped that first stone tool. Only a fool can fail to read the lesson that is written in our story. An emphasis on external power carries a built-in penalty. Read our novels, listen to our music, look at our art. Visit an insane asylum. Count the suicides. Count the graves of all the wars. Weigh the boredom, if you can—the emptiness, the frustration, the weariness, the desperate search for diversions. We have power over things: we can build bridges, houses, ships, planes. But have we been fulfilled as a people? Have we even found a measure of happiness? Why do we need pills to ease the knot in our guts? Is our yearning for the stars only an expression of inner poverty? Was there a toll bridge on the path we walked? Was there a hidden joker in the deck we opened?)

A way of life, yes.

But was it the only way?

What if man on Earth had never taken that first step?

What if he had turned down another trail, a different trail?

What if he had never chipped that first stone tool?

What other path had been open to him?

Consider the Merdosi, back in the mists of dawn on Sirius Nine. See them with their long ape-like arms, their naked bodies, their dark and intelligent eyes. See

them with the word-magic in their mouths, huddled together under a great white sun. . . .

They had taken a different turning. They had
started down a different trail.

What had it been?

Well, what were the key facts about the Merdosi
now? How had they behaved? What techniques had
they used?

Item: They had little or no visible material culture;
they didn't make *things*.

Item: They had a close and pivotal relationship
with some of the animals of their world, the Merdosini
and the saucer-eyed creatures that looked like tarsiers.
They seemed to control them.

Item: It was possible that they could influence
growth patterns to some extent. For example, those
hollow trees did not seem to be completely natural. And
perhaps they could grow other things. . . .

Item: They had been completely baffled by the
men from Earth. They had not been able to adjust to a
contact situation. They had been confused, upset,
afraid. They had attacked, first with the Merdosini and
then. . . .

Item: They had attacked their minds. They had
driven Charlie mad. While the men from Earth slept,
they had induced a sickness into their brains. They had
worked through their dreams. . . .

Item: The baffling thing about their culture was the
fact that there was nothing to *see*. All the visible clues
were lacking.

Item: What had the old man said? What had Volmay told him? "We will do what we must, all of us. We

cannot trust one another. My dreams told me that we might have a beginning-again, but the dreams are so strange since you have come. . . ."

Dreams.

Yes, and was there not a parallel among many of the primitive peoples of Earth, the peoples who had not yet been smothered by the mechanical monster? Did not all of them place great faith in dreams? Did they not use dreams to see into the future, to give meaning to their lives, to touch the unknowable? Did they not trust their dreams as sources of deep wisdom? Did not some of them, like the Iroquois, develop the idea of the subconscious long before Freud, and recognize that illness might be caused by a conflict between the inner man and supposedly rational thought?

(And how about our own dreams? Did we not speak of dreams as symbols of hope and ideals? And were not our attitudes toward them very much like those of the Merdosi toward artifacts? Weren't we great ones for giving lip-service to dreams? "Never lose your illusions, my boy! Always keep your dreams before you! But of course we must be practical, take a good course in Business Administration. . . .")

What did it all add up to?

Clearly, the Merdosi had developed a different aspect of the human personality. Their culture had centered on a different cluster of human possibilities. They had turned inward. They had tapped the hidden resources of the human mind. They worked in symbols, dreams, visions.

Telepathy? No, not quite. Rather, they seemed to have perfected a technique of projecting emotional states. That would account for their control over animals. That would account for what happened to Charlie—and to me.

But it must be more than that, far more. It must permeate every aspect of their lives. They must live in a world of symbolic richness, they must *see* the world in vivid colors, tones, shadings. They must be able to open their minds, share them. They must have techniques that we have never imagined—they must understand the growth of trees, the unfolding of life.

Yes, but the Merdosi were people too. They were not supermen. They were not idealized figments of the imagination. They were only different.

Wasn't there a hidden price-tag on their way of life too? What would the characteristics of such a culture have to be?

Obviously, there were certain advantages. There would be a closeness with other people, a harmony with life. Above all, there would be a kind of inner security, a peace. But the technique of dream interpretation depended in the final analysis on a static, unchanging society. Dreams did not come out of nowhere. As long as nothing changed, the old ways would work—you could understand the dreams, rely on them, trust the ancient commands they gave you.

But if you started to dream about a spaceship?

Or strange men with rifles?

Or men and women with alien customs?

Wouldn't the single basic fear of a secure society be the threat of insecurity, of change? What could you do when your dreams held no answers?

You would fear the coming of strangers with a dark,

cold terror. They would strike at the very roots of your existence. How could you possibly trust them when all they offered were *words*?

Words were not enough.

Contact was not enough—indeed, it might be fatal.

Protestations of friendliness were not enough.

I know what I must do.

The way is plain.

But can I trust myself, and all the things that have made me what I am? Is the bridge strong enough to hold us both?

It was no good trying to put it off. It had to be done. The next move was up to him.

Monte spent one last night in his cave, resting. Then he walked out into another of the glorious mornings of Sirius Nine, ate some of the pemmican he had prepared, and drank some water. He was ready.

He felt a certain affection for the little cave, and the symbolism of the place was not lost on him. Apart from that, he had always loved the high places. He was convinced that there were two basically different kinds of people— those who were drawn to the lowlands and those who found rest only in the mountains. If he could have his life to live over again, he decided, he would live more of it in the mountains where the air was clear and a man could touch the sky.

He looked down upon the green grasslands that rolled away to the darker green and yellow that lined the river. It *was* peaceful here, despite everything that had happened. Even the air seemed less irritating, and the rawness had left his throat. Could he not just once live up to the best that was in him, no matter what the cost?

Man had met man for the first time. The patterns of future history might well be determined by what happened here. And the universe was huge, swimming with islands of life. There was more at stake here than even the destinies of Earth and Walonka. There were other worlds, other men. Man had need of all the friends he could find, and one day he too would be judged.

Monte shrugged. It was a lot to ask of any one man. But perhaps it always came down to just one man, one decision, in the end. . . .

He grinned at the crumpled pieces of the spacesuit, still heaped on the rocky ledge. He wouldn't be needing them any longer.

He started down the trail.

He was amused at his self-styled role as a man of destiny. He was well aware that he was not the ideal man for the part. It was too bad, he thought wryly, that he could not have walked naked from the cave. That would have been a dandy symbol, a real corker, the very stuff of legends.

Unhappily, he couldn't risk the sunburn; he needed his clothes.

A parboiled hero! There was one for the books.

He walked on through the tall grasses, stroking his beard, smiling to himself.

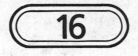

16

ONTE CROSSED THE river without incident. He retraced his steps to the clearing where he and Charlie had pitched their camp and was surprised to find it just as they had left it. Somehow, he had expected it to show the same changes he sensed in himself. That terrible day in the rain—surely that had been a million years ago, in another time, another age. . . .

He stopped only long enough to pick up his pipe and tobacco. He clamped the pipe between his teeth and savored the delicious smoke. If they ever stood him against a wall before a firing squad, he thought, he would ask for a last pipe.

It was all very strange, just as life itself was strange. It hadn't been very long ago that he had given up his pipe for fear of frightening the natives. Now, when he was about to walk the same path he had walked before, the pipe no longer mattered.

He had learned something, at least.

The externals didn't count.

He moved into the forest. The great trees closed in around him, whispering with activity, but he ignored them. He went on to the field where he had first glimpsed Volmay so long ago—where he had offered him food and seen the first of the Merdosini. He found the path which led into the woods, the dark path that for him would always hold the echoes of blackness and rain and the wind that swept the root of the world.

He located the hollow tree.

Volmay was sitting in front of it, his naked body gleaming in a fugitive patch of sunlight. His old head had fallen forward on his striped chest. He was asleep.

Dreaming?

As soon as Monte stepped into view, Volmay stirred and opened his eyes.

"Hello, Volmay."

"Monte. I speak your name. I dreamed that you would come."

"You did not wait for me."

Volmay smiled. "I waited here."

"I came as soon as I could."

"Yes. I knew that you would come. I wanted you to come. And yet I did not know—do not know——"

"What?"

"Whether it is good. I am an old man; I am confused. Nothing seems certain to me. I am very sorry about the—other."

"That is done."

"Perhaps." Volmay frowned; deep lines stood out on

his face. "I am sorry about all of the others. But I am only one man." He groped for words. He looked very tired.

"We are alike, you and I. We have both tried to do things that are hard for us to do. It is never easy to act alone. It is easier to flow with the tide, is that not so?"

"There are times when a man must swim against the current. I am ashamed that it took me so long. I was afraid."

"But you came to me. And now I have come to you."

The old man sighed. "It is not enough."

"No, we two can do nothing. I know that. I have come to—offer—myself."

The old man stood up. He looked at Monte with dark, sad eyes. "I do not understand your words."

"Sometimes a battle cannot be won by fighting. There are men of my people who found that out long before I was born. Sometimes a fight can only be won by a sacrifice, a surrender."

"That is a strange idea."

"Volmay, your people can see into my mind, is that not so?"

"If it is your wish. They cannot do it against your will."

"It *is* my will. I offer myself to them. I will hold back nothing. I want them to examine me. I want them to see for themselves what I am."

"And what are you, Monte?"

He laughed. "I am a man. I hope that is enough."

Volmay turned away. "How can you trust us, after what we have done? I can promise nothing. I do not know what will happen to you."

Monte sat down before the entrance to the hollow tree. It was warm in the sunlight. He refilled his pipe and puffed on it until the tobacco caught. "It seems to me that my people came here to you, not the other way around. We are the intruders. This is your world. It is only right that I should be on trial here, as you would be on trial if you came to our world. That is the way of things. I will accept your verdict."

The old man sat down beside him. "You will have no choice."

"I have already made my choice."

"I do not know. We are so very different. . . ."

"Are we? I thought so, once. But the first step must be taken. One of us must have faith. Or else——"

"What?"

"I have not the words to tell you."

"There will be—unhappiness?"

"More than that, Volmay. There are forces at work here that we are powerless to stop, you and I. Our two peoples have met. We will never be entirely separate again; this I know. We two are the beginning of a long, long story. We will not live to see the end of it—perhaps it will never end. If we can trust each other, we can be friends. If we fear each other, we must be enemies."

"Perhaps it was wrong of you to come. We did not ask you here."

"Who is to say? It may be that one day your children's children will be thankful that we came to you. In any event, we are here."

"Do *you* think we will ever be thankful that you came?"

"I do not know. That is the truth."

"You are very strange. Why *did* you come here? It must have been a long, hard journey."

"Why do you dream in the sun? Why do you live in a hollow tree? We are what we are. My people, Volmay—

they are a restless people. They have always been restless. To us, the stars were a challenge. Can you understand that?"

"The stars?" Volmay smiled. "The stars are the stars. They have always been there to light the darkness. But sometimes, at night, when the world is still, I have climbed high into the trees and looked at them and wondered. . . ."

"You do understand."

"I am not sure. I have always felt closest to the stars when I was alone, not moving. I have always felt closest to the stars when the night wind touched my face. Can you get nearer to the stars than that?"

"I don't know. How can I explain——"

"Yes. Exactly. Words—they are nothing. But, Monte, I must ask something of you. I do not know so many things."

"I will try to answer you."

He smiled an old, tired smile. "How can you trust yourself? You know nothing of your own mind. How can you know what my people will see in you? Your dreams. . . ."

"There is no other way."

Volmay looked at him. "There is hope. Yes. You survived an attack on your mind—you were strong enough to withstand it. That is surprising. There is something in you that carried you through. There is hope in that."

"I'd like to know myself what that something is."

"Yes. It is good for a man to know himself; I cannot imagine living otherwise. But my people are afraid. It will be very hard for them *not* to find evil in you. Do you understand that?"

"I understand. We are the same way, when we are afraid."

"And you are not afraid any longer?"

"I'm scared to death. But I'm more afraid of not trying."

"You will be very helpless, my friend. I would not want to be the cause of more harm coming to you."

"You have agreed that there is no other way."

"That is true."

"Then you must take me to the village and explain to them. Or if the time is wrong for the village, take me to the men."

Volmay looked at him with new interest. "You have learned about us."

He felt an odd thrill of pride, as though he had been given a professional compliment.

"Very well." The old man looked up into the trees. He squinted his eyes as though concentrating. He did not speak for a long minute. Monte followed his gaze and saw one of the little reddish-brown animals hiding in the branches, its huge eyes peering down at Volmay. He only caught a glimpse of the creature before it disappeared.

"I have sent a message," Volmay said. "All will be ready."

"Thank you."

The old man stood up and moved toward the tree. "We will eat together now. Then we will sleep. In the morning, we will go."

Monte followed him into the hollow tree.

It was high noon when they reached the village. The white furnace of the sun hung suspended in the middle of the sky, as though reluctant to move on. The eroded brown rock walls of the canyon reflected the light like smudged and

ancient mirrors. The waterfall at the head of the canyon was
an oasis of coolness, and the silver-flecked stream that
snaked across the canyon floor looked familiar and eternal
and inviting.

The cave-eyes of tunnels and rock shelters watched
them from the gray and brown rock faces of the cliffs.

In a sense, everything was just as it had been before—
and yet it was all different, completely different. There were
no children playing down along the river, no people going
about the seemingly aimless tasks of everyday living.

There was an air of taut expectancy in the village.

There was an aura of fear and suspicion and waiting.

The Merdosi had built a great fire on a ledge of rock
that jutted out over the canyon. They had all gathered
around the leaping flames in a circle of naked bodies and
dark, staring eyes.

Monte followed Volmay up a twisting trail. He could
not face the eyes that watched him. He looked at his feet
and walked steadily forward.

He felt naked, exposed, alone.

He could find nothing in himself to cling to, nothing to
help him.

He was beyond comfort, beyond science, beyond reason.

He was on trial, on trial before an alien judge and an
alien jury. He did not know their standards of right and
wrong, guilt or innocence. He did not even know what he
had done, or had not done. He did not know what he was.

And through him all the people of Earth were on trial.
Who was he to offer himself as the representative of a
world? Surely, there were better men. . . .

But if you really knew all there was to know about any man on Earth, would you invite him into your home?

He walked through the circle of eyes and stood with his back to the flames. It was very hot. He did not know whether or not he could stand it.

A young man with vertical blue stripes painted on his naked chest stood before him. He held out a gourd that was filled with a dark and fragrant liquid.

"Drink," the man said. "Drink and let your mind be open. It is the way."

Monte lifted the gourd to his lips and drank the stuff down. It tasted like heavy wine.

The fire blazed beneath him. The circle of eyes pressed closer, closer. . . .

The sky began to spin.

I will not hide. I will let them in. I want them to know, to see, to share. . . .

Black darkness and white light, all mixed up together.

Eyes.

They were in his mind, staring.

17

KNOCK KNOCK.
    "Who's there?
Art.
"Art who?"
Art Ifact!
(Laughter.)
WHAT IS HAPPENING TO ME? WHO AM I?
*There. There you are. See? You are still Monte Stewart.
I am Monte Stewart. When the mind is confronted with
something totally new it interprets it in terms of an ana-
logue. . . .*
    IS THIS AN ANALOGUE?
Call it what you will. Look. Listen.
    Question: Is this what you have hidden all your life,
kept sealed up inside you?
    Answer: Yes. I am ashamed. I was ashamed.
    (Laughter.)
    Q: Don't you know how small it is, how trivial?
    A: I didn't know.

Q: You know so much and so little. Are these the names you are trying to show us? Judas? Pizarro? Hitler?

A: Those are some of the names.

Q: Einstein? Tolstoy? Gandhi?

A: Those are some of the names.

(Snapshot: An ugly mushroom cloud, shadows pressed into concrete.)

Q: That is the hydrogen bomb?

A: Not that one. Only an atomic bomb. We used it twice.

(Snapshot: A beagle puppy in an animal shelter. A kid with big round eyes. The puppy wags its white-flagged tail.)

Q: Merdosini?

A: Only a pet.

Music.

Q. What is that?

A: *Swan Lake. The Original Dixieland One-Step. Stardust. John Henry. Scheherazade. The Streets of Laredo.*

Q: What is anthropology?

A: The study of man.

(Laughter.)

Q: What is this Exhibit A you keep thinking about?

A: It is evidence in a trial.

Q: A trial?

A: In a court of law.

Q: Law?

CONFUSION. A MAN IS INNOCENT UNTIL PROVEN GUILTY! A MAN HAS THE RIGHT TO CONFRONT HIS ACCUSER! THEY USED TO CHOP OFF YOUR HEAD IF YOU STOLE A RABBIT!

Q: Why did you come here, to Walonka?

A: We have been searching for men like ourselves.

Q. Why?

A: I don't know. We gave each other many reasons. Perhaps because the universe is vast and man is small.

Q: You needed us?

A: That was a part of it. And there was the excitement. . . .

Q: Like music?

A: Like music.

(A child's thought: "He's funny! He's funny!" And a mother-thought: "That's not nice!")

Q: Why do you smoke a pipe?

(Laugher. *His* laughter.)

Q: What is another world?

A: Earth is another world.

Q: Where is the Earth?

(Snapshot: Stars like fireflies in a great night. Empty miles lost in darkness. Round green islands floating, shining through necklaces of white clouds.)

A: It is far away.

Q: There were people like us on your world once?

A: No, not like you.

Q: But people who did not live as you live?

A: Yes.

Q: Why do you call them primitive?

CHAOS. TARZAN SWINGS ON A VINE, FLEXING HIS BI-
CEPS. "ME MAN, YOU GIRL." A NEANDERTHAL SCRATCHES
HIS HIDE AND PEERS FROM HIS CAVE. A MAN DRESSED IN
SKINS, WORKING BY THE LIGHT OF A STONE LAMP, PAINTS ON
A ROCK WALL DEEP BENEATH THE EARTH. AN INDIAN PRAYS
TO THE SUN. AN OLD ESKIMO MAN CRAWLS OUT ON THE ICE
TO DIE.

Q: What happened to these people on your Earth?

A: Some were killed, hunted down like animals. Some were put on reservations. Some were only—changed.

Q: Will this not happen to us, if your people come?

A: No! No! I don't think so.

Q: Why?

A: We have changed, we have grown up.

Q: Have you?

A: There are laws!

Q: Ah, we know that word! Who made the laws?

A: We did.

Q: What is progress? Your head is full of it.

A: I don't know. A word. Medicine. Ethics. Space-ships. . . .

Q: What is it like not to know yourself, to be empty inside? What is it like to be uncertain and afraid?

A FLASH OF RED. ANGER. REBELLION.

A: Physician, heal thyself!

(Laughter.)

Q: You admire your people?

(Pause.)

A: Sometimes.

Q: You think they are good, your people?

A: Sometimes.

Q: When?

A: Your questions have no answers! We are not perfect. We have done the best we could. We have tried!

Q: You admire our people, the Merdosi?

A: Sometimes.

Q: When?

A: When you come out of your shells, when you take a chance, when you don't take the easy way!

Q: When we are like you?

A: Perhaps. But that is because I don't really know you!
A man cannot admire what he does not understand. You
have hidden yourselves from me!

Q: And if a man understands, then he admires?

A: Not necessarily. But if he truly understands, he may
find compassion. He may even find love.

Q: Or hate?

A: That is possible. But there is hope. . . .

Q: Ah! You would like to see into our minds, to understand us?

A: Yes! Of course! But I haven't finished telling you
about my people. I have hardly begun! You don't know us
yet. I haven't told you about Plato and baseball, poets and
beer, Caesar and the Rocky Mountains, artists and Aztecs! I
haven't told you about science——

Q: You are wrong. We have seen all these things. It is
only that you don't remember—not all of our questions are
shaped into words. We know you now. But would you like
to know us?

A: Yes. But you can't possibly know my people yet! I
haven't done them justice. . . .

A KNIFE IN MY BRAIN, CUTTING THEM OFF. IT IS ALL
CHANGING. I AM GOING OUT. . . .

WAIT!

COME BACK!

IT IS OVER, IT IS OVER.

NO!

I CAN SEE, IT IS BEGINNING. . . .

I am not myself, but I am a man.
(What long arms you have, Grandpa!)

Is this what freedom means?

I am standing on the roof of the world. There are leaves all around me, red leaves and green leaves, and they draw a line across the sky. There is a cool breeze kissing my face; the air is clean and spiced with the smells of living things. The big sky arches above me. The sun is white and near and friendly.

There are birds nesting in the high branches: brown and yellow birds that sing with the sheer joy of being alive. Every leaf is new-minted, every line in the bark of age-old trees is unique.

Nothing has changed. This is where peace reigns supreme. It has always been so, from the beginning of time. It will always be here, waiting for me.

I dive from the top of the world. The blood races in my veins. I smile; who could keep from smiling? I rush through the cool green air, reach out with my strong right hand, catch a branch. It gives under my weight, but I swing in a great arc—forward and down, so fast that I can hardly breathe! My left hand breaks my fall and I swing on my long arm, swing out and down. . . .

(Look, Ma, I'm flyin'!)

I rest on a gnarled limb in the middle ranges, sealed off from the sky above and the land below. There is water here, standing in dark little hollows in the wood. And there is food: blue eggs in neat, round nests, red berries on thorny vines, combs of honey clouded in buzzing insects.

This is where a man belongs. This is where he finds his strength. This is where the good dreams are born.

There is no need to think, to analyze. It is enough to feel, to *be*. A man is not alone. He is a part of everything he

sees; he shares in the harmony of the open sky and the bud-
ding land and the thrusting trees. He is in the crystal rivers
that flow from dark mountain ranges, in the orange fires that
warm the night, in the air that whispers over waving grasslands.

I love this place. I am grateful for what it is. I am grateful too that it was given to me, for the Sun Shadows built
our world well, and built it to last forever. . . .

It was long ago and it was yesterday. It was in the beginning and it is now.

The Sun Shadows looked down on Walonka and were
sorry that it was lonely. They walked out on the Edge, where
it is neither night nor day, and there they found the Moon
Shadows. Together, hot and white and cold and silver, they
danced beneath the stars.

They made the Merdosi, born of the sun and the moon
in a shelter of stars. They carried them to Walonka. They
gave Walonka to the Merdosi and Merdosi to Walonka.

"Live under the sun," the Sun Shadows said. "Look up
and know that we are watching. Look down and see our
Shadows walking across your land. That is the way it will be,
forever."

"Live under the moon," the Moon Shadows said.
"Look up and know that we are watching. Look down and
see our Shadows walking across your land. That is the way it
will be, forever."

The sun and the moon did not forget. They always
watch us from our sky. The Merdosi did not forget. We
have honored the Shadows of the Sun and the Shadows of

the Moon, and we have kept Walonka as they gave it to us.
We have been careful. . . .

A dream?

I am a man. A man spends half of his life with his eyes
open and half of his life lost in dreams. The two go together.
A man cannot live without his dreams and a dream cannot
live until it is acted upon.

It is good to dream, to refresh myself. There is wisdom
in dreams. If you dream in the afternoon, the Sun Shadows
speak to you. If you dream at night, the Moon Shadows
speak to you. And if you can dream on the Edge. . . .

My dreams speak truth to me always. They tell me what
I really want to do. And what I really want to do is *right*, for
am I not a man?

Of course, sometimes a dream is not clear. It must be
interpreted. There are Merdosi who are skilled in such
things. And twice a year we all dream together. . . .

It is dangerous to change. When the old ways are left
behind, the dreams are confused. It is hard to know what is
right.

It is wise to accept the world that was given to us. Our
lives have been comfortable. Each of us in his time repeats a
cycle that goes back to the Beginning.

And yet. . . .

Sometimes the dreams are strange. There are longing
dreams. There are dreams that speak of unknown countries.
There are restless dreams. When a man wakes from such a
dream, he is unhappy, he is filled with a sense of something
missed, something lost. . . .

It is better to ignore such dreams.

It is better to keep things as they are, forever.

(Ask me no questions. . . .)

I am a boy.

I have lived my life in the village with the women and the old men. I have played down by the river. I have not told the Elders about *all* of my dreams, for I am ashamed. I have been happy, I suppose. But there are times. . . .

I have seen the men come into the village. I have sensed the thrill in the air. I have watched, sometimes. . . .

I have watched the men go back into the great forest, where the trees grow tall. How I have wanted to go with them!

My time is coming. I am *almost* a man.

They will build a great fire on the ledge that looks down over the river. They will bring us together, four boys and four girls. We will drink together, and the Elders will look into my mind. I hope they don't see everything!

If we are fit, we will be taken to the Place—four boys and four girls. There we will stay alone with the Sun Shadows and the Moon Shadows. We will stay alone until we are no longer boys and girls

Renna has dreamed of me. I know she has, for she has told me so. And when the moon is full, and we are at the Place. . . .

I am afraid, but I can hardly wait.

I want to be a man!

And later, much later, I can go into the great forest alone and find my tree. . . .

*   *   *

I see—myself!

I come out of the sky in a round metallic thing that lands in a clearing. I step out into the air of Walonka. I sneeze.

How strange I look with my short arms and funny clothes, clutching my rifle! I am full of questions, full of strange smells. My mind is cold.

I am an alien.

I walk toward the forest. I never look up toward the roof of the world. I am busy with schemes, plans, subterfuges.

I am different.

I walk toward the Merdosi. I am something new, something unknown, something dangerous.

What do I want, with my cold, closed mind?

What do I want, with my words that are only words?

I am Change.

I am to be feared; I cannot be trusted.

I keep coming, keep coming, keep coming. . .

Go away, go away!

I keep coming, keep coming. . .

Go back, go back!

I keep coming, keep coming. . . .

Knock knock.

"Who's there?"

BLACKNESS!

18

MONTE STEWART OPENED his eyes. At first, he was confused. The black nothingness of oblivion was gone, but it had been replaced by a gray, featureless gloom that was not much more informative. He felt a hard surface under him. He reached over with his hand and touched rock. He sat up, squinting. He felt dizzy and faint, but there seemed to be a lighter patch of gray to his right. . . .

Of course! He was in one of the village caves. He had passed out during the trial, if that was the right word for it, and. . . .

It all came back with a rush.

He leaped to his feet and ran toward the entrance to the cave. He stuck his head out, grinning like an idiot. The village was asleep around him, asleep and strangely beautiful in the first pale light of the dawn. The waterfall was a murmur of silver, the winding river a ribbon of glass. The forest was deep and dark and inviting.

He was on the Edge, where it was neither night nor day.

There was no fear in him now. There was no worry, no uncertainty.

He did not have to ask any questions.

He *knew*.

(Had he not seen into their minds, as they had seen into his? He knew the decision of the Merdosi as surely as they themselves did.)

He was free.

More than that, he had won—won for all of them.

He was frankly surprised at the outcome, and yet it had a certain inevitability about it. He was surprised and he was proud. He was proud of himself, proud of his people, proud of the Merdosi. And he was grateful—grateful for the meaning that had been given to his life.

He had lived his life in the conviction that understanding was possible between people. He had lived his life in the belief that hope was possible between men and women. He had lived his life in the belief that hope was not an obsolete word. How many men are given such a dramatic proof of the codes by which they live?

The verdict?

It was not a simple thing, not a matter of being guilty or not guilty. (What was the crime, what was the law?)

It was rather a matter of *acceptance*.

The Merdosi had accepted him as a man, as a human being that was neither all bad nor all good. They had accepted his people for what they were, seeing in them a fundamental kinship with themselves. They had recognized the differences and respected them.

Perhaps they would have preferred never to have met the men from Earth. But the men from Earth had come.

The Merdosi, at the very least, were prepared to make the best of a bad bargain.

They were willing to give the strangers the benefit of the doubt.

They loved their world the way it was, and yet they were big enough to know that they were not perfect. They had things to learn, just as did the men from Earth. It would take time, and the way would not be easy, but they were ready to try. They did not know where the new road might lead; there would be many new dreams. But surely, if all men walked the road together, it would be a good road. . . .

Monte stood for a long time on the Edge, waiting for the night to end and the day to begin. He watched the stars winking out one by one. He sensed the silent thunder of the dawn.

The Merdosi had looked into his heart and mind, and they had trusted him. But what of his own people? What would they do to the world of Walonka in the years to come? Could *he* trust the men of Earth?

If the Merdosi could have faith in the aliens, could he have none?

But it would take more than faith.

There was work to be done.

He walked down the trail that wound down to the canyon floor, leaving the sleeping village behind him. There was no need to tell them he was leaving or where he was going; they already knew. He was free to go, just as he was welcome to stay.

He walked along the purling river.

Just as the great white sun flamed behind the mountains, he vanished among the trees of the waiting forest.

* * *

It was late afternoon when he reached the little clearing. The battered tents still stood. The blank-faced spacesuit helmets still lay where they had fallen. The charred black logs of the dead fire were still in place.

Monte shivered, despite the heat of the day. He was not alone here. He was surrounded by watching eyes, eyes of the living and eyes of the dead. He was engulfed in two sets of memories—his and those of the Merdosi. He was at once the explorer setting foot in a strange and unknown land and the native who stared and feared and wondered.

He sat down on a rock to rest, cupping his bearded chin in his hands. The problem, really, was the same as it had always been. The problem was communication, getting through to people. First it had been the Merdosi. Now it was his own people.

His own people. . . .

A wave of homesickness swept through him, more intense than any he had ever known. This was not his world, could never be his world. He was hungry for the sights and sounds he knew, hungry for a sun that was not a white furnace filling an alien sky. He had done his job, hadn't he? Surely they could expect nothing more of him. He had only to signal the waiting ship, and go home.

(Home, the loveliest word in the language—in any language! See the shining snow on the Rockies, the green of the mountain meadow in spring, the friendly books that lined his office. Have a cup of steaming coffee, sleep in his own bed, have a classic bull session with the boys. And who was looking after the flowers that Louise had planted?)

That wasn't all, either. He would be famous, wouldn't he? He would be a big shot, a hero. Didn't every man have a hankering to be a wheel, even when he laughed at the wheels he knew? He would be a Success, a cornball dream come true. He could write his own ticket. He could be the top man in his field.

He got up, filled his pipe, and went to work. He straightened up the devastated tents, built a fire, and cooked a meal. Then he dug out the voice-typer and set it up by his cot. He lined up a supply of tobacco, arranged the portable light, and sat down to think.

This was going to be the most important piece of writing he had ever done in his life. Quite possibly, it was the most important piece of writing that *anyone* had ever done.

He tried to remember them, those people he must reach with his inadequate words. He tried to think of them as individuals. Admiral York—not an easy man to sell. Tom Stein and Janice; their memories of the Merdosi were anything but pleasant. Don King, a cynic with small use for dreams. Mark Heidelman. The secretary-general.

And there were so many others: politicians, reporters, hordes of self-styled experts.

How would he himself have received the story of the Merdosi if he had never come to Sirius Nine? He pictured himself sitting in his university office, his beard neat and trim, his eyes skeptical. He saw a student come crashing into his sanctum, all full of the wonderful story of the Merdosi. He could almost hear the biting sarcasm of his own comments. . . .

He stared blanky at the voice-typer. Outside the lighted tent, he could feel the darkness of the world around him. Where were the words that could tell his story?

What could he say about the precedent he had tried to set, without sounding like a pompous idiot? How could he tell them what he had learned, without sounding like a romantic fool? How could he make it clear to everyone that this was a matter of life and death, a question of ultimate survival? How could he show them the enormity of the sacrifice the Merdosi were making by permitting the strangers to come among them? How could he explain the lesser sacrifice his people must make in return, a sacrifice of restraint, of wisdom, of humility?

He could only tell his story to the best of his ability. He could only use the feeble words he knew. He could only hope that the truth was good enough.

What was the story he had to tell?

It was a simple story, really.

There were no primitive supermen. (Wasn't that what we secretly longed for? Didn't we want god-like beings who would shoulder our responsibilities for us? Didn't we want a benevolent sorcerer who might wave a magic wand over our world?)

There were no bestial savages. (Wasn't that what we secretly wanted too? A nice evil monster that we could handle, instead of the monsters we all had within us? A bug-eyed tentacled beast that we could focus all of our little hates upon?)

It was a shame. There were no supermen. (Lay my burden down!) There were no monsters. (Kill the witch!)

There were just people.

It was just a story of people who had taken a different turning on the pathway of life. Just a story of human beings—more advanced and less advanced, better and worse. Just a story of the Merdosi, who had been afraid to give their trust—until now. A story of a people ready to learn, and to teach. And a story of the Edge, of Sun Shadows, and Moon Shadows and a shelter of stars. . . .

A story of how man met man, and wanted him for a friend.

He thought it was a good story, a story of promise, a story of beginnings. But he could not write the ending. That was up to the men of Earth.

He went to work.

It took him two days to tell his story.

When he had finished, he carefully arranged the machine cylinders and the manuscript on the table by the voice-typer. He took out his battered notebook and placed that on top of the pile. He had concealed nothing, held nothing back.

As soon as the time was right, he called the reconnaissance sphere on the portable radio equipment. It was there, as it was once each day, waiting for his call.

He talked fast, telling Ace what he had done and where the materials were. He told him what he was going to do and that he was in good shape. He made a few requests: tobacco, food, clothing. Then he cut the contact. He could not bear to listen to Ace's familiar Texas voice; it was too much like home.

And he couldn't go home, not yet.

He might never get home again.

He knew that if he ever returned to the ship he was through. Admiral York would never permit him to come back to Walonka, and he would never leave him behind if he had any choice. And Monte knew that it would be very easy to let himself be persuaded. Once he was on the ship it would be easy to convince himself that he wasn't needed here, that his job was done.

It wasn't done, of course. It was just beginning. It wasn't enough to blithely make contact with a people. What was needed was a bridge, a bridge of sympathy and understanding. He would have to be that bridge. There was no one else.

One day, the ships from Earth would come again.

He had to be ready.

He changed his clothes and loaded his pockets with tobacco. He took nothing else. He left the tent, walked across the clearing, and entered the dark woods.

He did not look back.

There were open spaces in the forest where the blue sky showed through, but he averted his eyes. He did not want to see the gray sphere come down. He did not want to think of the great invisible ship that was his last link with home.

He walked on toward the hollow tree, where old Volmay would be waiting.

They had a lot of dreaming to do together.

After the Beginning

I T TOOK FOUR years.

They were long years, and busy years. Monte, caught in the web of one culture, could well imagine what was happening in the other. It would have taken the spaceship about eleven months to reach Earth from Sirius Nine. It would take it another eleven months to come back again. Therefore the people of Earth had had two years and a couple of spare months in which to make up their minds.

That was about par for the course. How had the decision been reached? With cartoons and editorials and public debates? Or by secret discussions within the United Nations?

Well, no matter.

The men of Earth *had* to come back, that was certain. But *how* they would come, and for what purpose. . . .

That was something else again. That was the worry that nagged at Monte for many long days and nights.

It had been a strange four years. There had been the excitement, the thrill of exploring a new and unknown civilization. (He knew now how they had felt, those men who had first seen the ruins of the Maya, the hidden tombs of ancient Egypt, the Eskimo shamans in the long Arctic night!) And there had been the loneliness, the very special kind of loneliness that a man knows when he is cut off from his kind. He could never truly be a part of the Merdosi way of life; he was sealed away from it by years of alien experiences. He longed for the sights and sounds of Earth, and yet he was no longer quite a man of Earth either.

Change was always hard.

He had made new friends, and Volmay in particular was as remarkable a man as any he had ever known. But Monte missed his old friends, the men and women who had shared that other life with him. The loss of Louise was a hollow ache within him.

Perhaps he was just growing old. He was getting to the age where a man seeks a return, a link with his own past, a closing of the circle of life.

And there had been one real crisis.

It seemed very obvious to him now, and he wondered that he had not thought of it before. It was inherent in the situation. When the Merdosi looked into his mind, they saw more than his personality, more than a reflection of the character of his people. They saw the possibility of their own destruction—and they saw a new kind of knowledge.

Artifacts, for them, had always been a sort of confession of weakness. But they could not help recognizing their own weakness when contrasted with the men of Earth. They could see the advantages of weapons, just as Monte could see the advantages of a technique of projecting emotions. If you combined the two, you had a defense of sorts.

Just in case.

Some of the younger Merdosi men began to experiment. They were able to bypass millenniums through the medium of his mind. It was absurd to imagine that they could build themselves a missile with a nuclear warhead, of course; Monte could not have done it himself. But bows and arrows were something else again.

It was pathetic, but it had the seeds of destruction in it.

It made the situation just that much more critical. An arrow can kill as surely as a bomb or a bullet. And a death now could only invite retaliation. If that happened, Monte's whole life was reduced to an ironic joke.

Four strange and worried years. . . .

It was with mixed emotions that Monte watched the coming of the ship, one spring day.

The monstrous ship filled the sky, blotting out the sun, making no attempt at concealment.

(A show of force?)

Landing spheres detached themselves from the mother ship and started down. Monte counted twenty of them. They glittered like ominous bubbles in the sunlight.

They landed.

With a sinking heart, Monte watched the soldiers climb out.

They lined up in little rows, like toy soldiers on parade. Behind them, in a protected pocket, stood six men who were not in uniform. That, at least, was encouraging. Monte would have given a lot for a good pair of field glasses.

Volmay smiled a tired old smile. "They have come to rescue you from the monsters, my friend."

"It looks that way."

"What will we do?"

"Will you go and speak to the other men, Volmay? Tell them to get ready. Tell them to have patience. Tell them that there has been a misunderstanding."

"I will do that. And you?"

Monte shrugged. "If they're so dead-set on doing it, I guess I'll go down there and let them rescue me."

"Alone?"

"That would be best, I think."

"Will they listen to what you have to say?"

"They'll listen. They'll listen unless they're prepared to shoot me on sight."

"You will be careful?"

"Yes."

"I wish you well. We will be waiting."

Monte clenched his fists and clamped his empty pipe between his teeth. He left the shelter of the trees and started across the field toward the soldiers.

* * *

The soldiers saw him coming. They stayed in formation, screening off the six civilians.

Monte walked up to them, his blood boiling. He put his hands on his hips, took a deep breath, and spat out of the corner of his mouth. He stood there, looking them up and down: skinny, ragged, bearded, his eyes as cold as ice.

"Get the hell out of my way," he said diplomatically.

One of the soldiers sneezed.

A colonel stepped forward. "Try to be reasonable, sir. We know you've been through a lot. But we have a procedure to follow here——"

"Great!" Monte was getting madder by the minute. "If I may coin a phrase, colonel, we can do without your particular bull in this china shop. Let's get something straight, shall we? The Merdosi are back there in the trees, watching every move you make. Right now they're friendly. More than that—they're trusting us. But you've got to get these soldiers out of here."

The officer flushed. He made a desperate effort to salvage his dignity, but a sneeze caught him unawares. "I have my orders——"

"Just a minute, please." A tall man in civilian clothes pushed through the line of soldiers. His hair was grayer than Monte remembered it, but he had the same smiling eyes. "Monte, is it really you?"

"Bob!" Monte laughed and clapped him on the shoulder. "Bob Cotten! My God, the last time I saw you——"

"The Triple-A meetings in Denver, wasn't it? It's been a long time, too long. Man, you look like a ghost. What have they been doing to you?"

"Bob, have you got some authority around here?"

Bob Cotten grinned. "Well, I'm the new anthropologist in charge of making contact with the natives. I guess I've sort of got your old job."

"For two cents I'd let you start from scratch. Boy, am I glad to see you! Can't you get this damned army out of here? Everything's okay if we don't mess it up now."

"You're sure?"

"Yes. You want me to sign it in triplicate?"

"That won't be necessary, Monte. Your word is good enough for me. But you'll have to talk to the big boys."

"Who'd you bring with you? The P.T.A.?"

"Not quite. The secretary-general sent along a committee of five. (We know how much you love committees, Monte.) They've got a big fancy title—something about Extraterrestrial Relations, which sounds highly immoral—but they're okay. One person each from the United States, Russia, England, China, and India. They won't give you any trouble, once they get a go-ahead from you. But the way things were left here, it's understandable that no one wanted to take chances."

"I told you everything's okay." Monte turned to the man in uniform. "If the colonel will be good enough to stand aside. . . ."

The officer waved his hand. "Sure, sir. Glad to have you back, Dr. Stewart."

Monte shook his hand. "Sorry I was so cantankerous, colonel. Buy you a drink later?"

The colonel sneezed and managed a smile. "I could use one."

Bob Cotton escorted him to the five waiting men.

They all had smiles of welcome on their faces.

Monte felt a great load lifting from his shoulders. He almost broke down and cried.

Everything was going to be all right.

Later that same afternoon, the first meeting took place between the two groups. It happened in a little clearing in the forest, not far from Volmay's tree.

On the face of it, the meeting wasn't very dramatic. It would have made a poor scene in a play, no matter how the music swelled behind it. Indeed, Monte thought, there were only two people left on two worlds who could really appreciate the enormity of what happened.

He himself was one.

Volmay was the other.

They stayed on the fringes now, gladly relinquishing the stage. But they were both remembering. Remembering that other meeting that had been only yesterday as worlds count time, and yet had been an eternity ago in some far lost age. . . .

Volmay had been standing there, frozen with fear, and the wolf-thing had padded across the leaves.

Monte had walked toward him, meat in one hand and berries in the other.

"Monte," he had said, pointing at himself. . . .

Had that been only yesterday, even as the worlds count time?

It was all so easy now.

Monte had led Bob Cotten and the U.N. committee to the clearing. They had left the soldiers behind and they were unarmed. The men of the Merdosi had been waiting, their bows and arrows tossed casually into the bushes.

One of the Merdosi men had stepped forward and shaken the hand of the man from India, smiling with pleasure at being able to show off his knowledge of the customs of Earth. "You are welcome among my people," he said in English.

"We have come in peace," said the man from India, proudly speaking a sentence he had learned in the Merdosi language. (Charlie's records, back on the ship, had been put to good use.) "I want you to meet my friends."

Simple.

Nothing to it.

Monte looked across at Volmay, and the old man solemnly winked at him.

That night, Monte slept alone in his tent. He was not quite ready to feel the steel of the ship around him. Outside, a small fire burned against the darkness of the hushed and silent world.

A light breeze began to blow, whispering through the trees its song of silvered rivers and sleeping grasslands and distant mountains. A fat yellow moon floated over the edge of the black forest.

Perhaps the Moon Shadows spoke to him as he slept; who can say?

For the dreams came to him again as they had come before into this tent in this clearing. The dreams came to him again, but this time they were different dreams: the dreams that come best when a man's work is done and he is alone.

Monte Stewart smiled in his sleep.

He was dreaming the best dream of all, the dream of the magic promise, the dream of going home.

Afterword

I T HAS BEEN nearly a quarter of a century since I wrote *Unearthly Neighbors*. As a matter of fact, there is one sense in which I didn't write *Unearthly Neighbors* at all— my title for the book was *Shoulder the Sky*. With my usual uncanny timing, another novel (not science fiction) was published under that name just before my book was due to come out. Hence, *Unearthly Neighbors*. To this day, I don't know whose title it was.

Although the point has seldom been noted, most of my novels begin in the present (the time during which the story was written) or in the near-future. For instance, my first novel (*Mists of Dawn*, 1952) opened in the present and went back into the past. My second (*Shadows in the Sun*, 1954) started in the present and stayed there. My third (*The Winds of Time*, 1957) began with an ordinary fishing trip in "present" Colorado; the aliens and the space scenes came later. *Unearthly Neighbors* was my fourth novel. If you have read this far, you know that the story opens in the near-future.

This may or may not have been a wise writing strategy, but at least I know why I utilized it. It is a technique more commonly employed in films than in written fiction and it amounts to this: anchor your story in a reality the reader or viewer can recognize first, and *then* bring on whatever marvels you may have up your sleeve. There was a time when science fiction did not enjoy the acceptance that it now has, and perhaps the most frequent criticism of the field was that it was purely escape fiction (it had nothing meaningful to say about *us* and the world we lived in) and that there were no *people* in science fiction—only machines. Stupid, of course, but there you are. I wanted to reach a wider audience, not just preach to the converted, and I thought that one way of doing this was to give readers characters with whom they could identify. I love good space opera—I grew up on it—but as a writer I wanted to try something else.

In my short stories and novelettes, published in magazines that were read by people who already knew and understood what science fiction was all about, I could take a lot for granted and go on from there. In my novels, however, I made an attempt to introduce my characters against relatively familiar backgrounds. I might or might not do the same today; we shall have to wait and see.

Which brings us to the revisions I have made in this edition of *Unearthly Neighbors*.

If you set a story in the "present," that is not a major problem. Assuming that you did your job right, that's the way it was and there is little more to be said unless you decide to "update" the story.

If you set a story in the near-future, that's a different bag of beans. The near-future *then* (when you wrote the story) turns into something perilously close to the present *now*. To coin a less-than-inspired phrase, a lot has happened during the last quarter of a century. It is one thing to predict space travel and quite another to anticipate the Beatles.

When I reread *Unearthly Neighbors*, it was obvious to me that the first three chapters had to be rewritten. The technological aspects of the story held up tolerably well, considering that I wrote it less than three years after the first Sputnik and more than a year before Yuri Gagarin orbited the Earth. I could have lived with the errors I made in that area. The mistakes that kicked me in the teeth were social.

Sure, the tone was off a little; the flavor was wrong. Sure, we all write lines that we itch to change. But the major problem was centered on the relationships between the male and female characters. I was chagrined to discover that there were sexist elements in my writing. They were unintentional, but they were undeniably there. That is primarily what I tried to fix, within the limits set by the structure of the story. If I were plotting the novel today, it would be a different expedition that set out for Sirius Nine.

There were two words that gave me trouble throughout the book. One was *man* and the other was *native*. I was using *man* in the generic sense, meaning humanity, but the constant reiteration of the word tends to fall like hammer thuds on modern sensitivities. I won't belabor the point here, but the tactic that I adopted was to make clear what my intentions were and then leave the word alone. If you cast the term into oblivion, this can result in some decidedly odd prose. A book entitled *The Evolution of Man* suddenly reappears as *Peoplekind in Metamorphosis*, and that really won't do unless you have a tin ear for words. (Recall that the word *evolution* is also taboo in some quarters.) There is a similar difficulty with *native*. The word is no longer used in anthropology because it carries negative connotations. People are not fond of being referred to as *natives*. There are too many past associations with *savage* or *ignorant*. What is a *native* anyhow, except someone who has been displaced or a person who happens to live elsewhere from the observer? As the old joke has it, "Everybody has to be someplace." Again, I tried to make my meaning clear—the *natives* are *people* who inhabit Sirius Nine—and then generally let the word stand.

You may possibly wonder why I did not simply go ahead and completely rewrite the entire novel. There were many reasons, but I will mention only three. First, I found—somewhat to my surprise—that I liked a lot of it the way it was. ("If it ain't broke, don't fix it.") Second, believe it or not, authors are among the things that change in a quarter of a century. Unless you are dead from the neck up, you don't have exactly the same outlook at fifty-five that you had when you were thirty. A good deal of experience gets in the way, and you start to argue with your own characters. That is apt to prove fatal to a novel, which must stand or fall within some consistent framework. Finally, I didn't want to cheat *too* much. There is always the temptation to throw in enough topical references so that the writer appears to have been omniscient. (No, I didn't insert the Beatles.)

I think we still have a long way to go in our attitudes toward extraterrestrial lifeforms. The popular polarities are neatly represented by *Close Encounters of the Third Kind* and John Carpenter's *The Thing*. In one, we virtually genuflect before godlike beings, and in the other we react with all the aplomb of a child dropped into a tub of rattlesnakes. We'll have to do better than that. (Yes, there's *E.T.*, but that poses yet another threat to humanity—a case of the terminal cutes.) With all due respect to Mr. Spock, it might be worth mentioning that we still have no anthropologist aboard the *Enterprise*. I would agree that anthropologists are not the sole curators of wisdom in the human race, but perhaps we could find room for one or two when the aliens really hit the fan.

I continue to believe that a part of our future lies Out There, just as I believe that a part of our future is situated Right Here. I also believe that we must understand ourselves before we can hope to interact intelligently with Others, whoever they may turn out to be. In my own mind, that's what *Unearthly Neighbors* is all about.

It's also a story, of course. I hope you enjoyed it.

Chad Oliver

April 1984
Austin, Texas